"A lot of things about you remind me of myself," Camp said softly. His eyes moved across her face in a leisurely, caressing way, and the pounding of Dusty's heart, which had begun with the brief playful struggle, abruptly changed to a light, rapid tripping. His arm around her waist was warmly pleasurable, the absent, tender motions of his hand upon her hair mesmerizing. She wanted him to go on looking at her, and touching her, in exactly that way forever. "The stubbornness, the stupid pride, the headstrong impulses...we're two of a kind, Dusty."

With her partial weight resting on his chest and her elbow her only support, his face was only inches below her. It was a beautiful face, strong and kind and open, a face she could see becoming part of her life, a man she could too easily come to rely upon....

ABOUT THE AUTHOR

Rebecca Flanders is a native of Georgia who began her writing career at age nine. She completed her first novel by the time she was nineteen and sold her first book in 1979. Rebecca's hobbies are oil and watercolor painting and composing and listening to music.

Books by Rebecca Flanders

HARLEQUIN AMERICAN ROMANCES
6-A MATTER OF TRUST
24-BEST OF FRIENDS
41-SUDDENLY LOVE
51-GILDED HEART
58-SECOND SIGHT
66-DESERT FIRE

HARLEQUIN PRESENTS
632-MORNING SONG
666-FALKONE'S PROMISE

HARLEQUIN ROMANCES
2623-A MODERN GIRL

These books may be available at your local bookseller.

For a list of all titles currently available, send your name and address to:

Harlequin Reader Service
P.O. Box 52040, Phoenix, AZ 85072-2040
Canadian address: P.O. Box 2800, Postal Station A,
5170 Yonge St., Willowdale, Ont. M2N 5T5

Desert Fire

REBECCA FLANDERS

Harlequin Books

TORONTO • NEW YORK • LONDON
AMSTERDAM • PARIS • SYDNEY • HAMBURG
STOCKHOLM • ATHENS • TOKYO • MILAN

Published August 1984

ISBN 0-373-16066-6

Printed in Canada

Chapter One

The flat desert highway was an unrelenting slash across the monotony of the barren night, and the restless shadows of the moon were her only companion as Dusty Macleod trudged ruthlessly onward. The tight green sheath was not made for walking, and neither were the high-heeled strapped sandals. Her feet were raw and probably bleeding, but Dusty grimly clenched her teeth against the pain, almost welcoming it. She deserved it. She had been played for the fool again and she deserved everything she got.

Dusty had started for the bus station only to discover that fifty dollars would get her a one-way ticket to nowhere, and then she had kept on walking. She hadn't relized what a stupid move that was until she had left the plastic oasis of Las Vegas far behind, and then innate stubbornness had refused to let her turn back. That had been some time ago. Traffic along the usually well traveled route was almost nonexistent except for an occasional semi or straggling vehicle headed toward the city, on the opposite side of the road. Dusty guessed it must be early morning, but she had no way of telling. Her watch—the elegant gold Pulsar that Peter had given her as an engagement present—now adorned the wrist of some nameless Las Vegas woman, and all that Dusty owned was stuffed into the canvas overnight bag slung over her shoulder. The rest of her luggage would be arriving at Peter's hotel suite sometime tomorrow, but Dusty would never see it again. Her own belongings—the treasures she had accumulated so proudly and painstakingly over the years, odd pieces of mismatched furniture, bric-a-brac, linens, even her record collection, and her small black-and-white television set—had all been disposed of for the move to Las Vegas. It had hurt Dusty to do that, for she had had so little in her life and had worked so hard to acquire what she did have, that she had formed an extraordinary, sentimental attachment to everything she could call her own. But Peter had insisted her meager possessions would be redundant and yes, tacky, in the midst of the splendor of his desert home, and she had reluctantly agreed. Now she blinked her eyes against a bitter salty blur and determined not to cry over all she had lost. She had started from scratch before and she would do it again. . . . She would *not* let one man, one low-life, one rash and contemptible mistake destroy her. She simply would not.

Dusty had not realized how exhausted she was until she heard the muted whine of faraway tires upon the echoing asphalt. She turned and saw the pinpoint headlights deceptively clear in the unbroken desert, seeming closer than they actually were. Her feet throbbed and her eyelids felt as though they were filled with sand, the shoulder strap of her bag had worn a blister across her bare skin and the muscle ached. If only some kind soul— some vacationing retirees or besotted honeymooners—would offer her shelter in the back seat of their car, a place to curl up and close her eyes while a powerful engine put steady miles between herself and Las Vegas. . . .

But it wasn't a car that approached, she saw after a time, but a pickup truck. Still, she remained poised hopefully, willing to accept anything, until the vehicle began to slow down and she saw what it contained. She turned abruptly and began walking again as the truck slowed to a crawl along the shoulder beside her.

"Hey, baby, looking good!"

"Where're you headin', doll?"

"Climb in, sweet piece, we're gonna have ourselves a *high* time!"

Whooping laughter, shouts and taunts, accompanied the crunch of creeping tires on the gravel shoulder beside her, and Dusty glared at the truck's occupants just once and kept on walking. Three boys, teenagers or very young men, hung out of the windows, jeering and grinning at her, all of them with bottles, so close now she could smell the stench of perspiration and cheap whiskey. Dusty was not frightened, only furious with herself. Here she was on a desert highway miles from anywhere, and what did she think she was doing? Where the hell did she think she was going? This wasn't New York, for heaven's sake, she couldn't just turn around and hail a cab. . . . She trudged angrily on, ignoring the suggestive taunts in her ear, biting her lip as she turned her foot on a loose stone and the strap of her sandal dug into her ankle.

"Come on, babe, don't be stingy! Let's take a little ride!"

One of the boys was climbing out of the window now, cheered on by his companions, hanging on to the doorframe and looping his foot over the truck bed with the grace of a drunken acrobat as he held out a half-empty bottle to her. "Want a little taste?" he invited with a sloppy grin. "You give me some of yours and I'll give you some of mine."

Their shouts of laughter continued as Dusty growled, "Get the hell away from me." She turned deftly and started walking the other way.

That was a smart trick, it worked well on narrow city streets crowded with traffic. On an empty desert highway, all the truck had to do was back up a few feet and stop, disgorging its occupants with lazy recklessness into a sauntering semicircle around her. Dusty felt the hairs on the back of her neck prickle in instinctive animalistic response to the threat closing in on her, the drunken grins flashing in the moonlight, the swaying gaits that disguised taut readiness, the crooning confident voices that sounded like a tribal chant as they moved in for the kill. And, animallike, she felt adrenaline surge, her own muscles tense, and fury, not fear, tasted like copper in the back of her throat.

With her senses, not her eyes, she saw one of them approach her from behind while the other two stood perfectly still about three feet away from her, emitting low-key danger in the confidence of their grins. Just as broad hands closed upon her shoulders, she whirled, jamming her heavy purse into the abdomen of her startled assailant and the spiked heel of her shoe into his kneecap. She had been aiming for the groin and she was furious that she had missed. She heard a stunned yelp, and caught one satisfied glimpse of the surprised and pained face before the other two were upon her and the jungle fight was on.

Rough hands grabbed and pushed, grunting things like, "Not nice, baby, we was only tryin' to be nice to you ... Come on, get in the truck, we're gonna have us a good time...."

Dusty clawed and kicked, her aim improving until one boy rolled to the ground screaming with pain, and the other two stopped playing and started fighting in earnest. Dimly she was aware of a bright light illuminating the entire scene and a roaring noise that had not been there before but she paid it scant attention, all senses now attuned to the fire of battle that was burning through her veins. Dusty was a street fighter from way back and she knew how to take care of herself—something for which these good-time boys had obviously not been prepared when they had spotted the sexy petite woman in the green sheath and spiked heels alone and defenseless on an empty highway. Her doubled fist sent one of them reeling, another went weak beneath the ruthless backward pressure she applied to his middle finger when he tried to grab her bodice. But then the other two were upon her. Her purse and her overnight bag were ripped from her shoulder and tossed into the bed of the pickup, and with a shriek of primal rage she released the hold she had upon the third. An arm clamped around her waist and began dragging her toward the truck, she doubled over and sank her teeth into a bony wrist, at the same time snatching her sharp heeled shoe from her foot. When the arm released her she used the shoe like a bludgeon, its pointed heel gouging hands and faces and warding off reciprocal blows. They were swearing angrily now, bleeding and sweating and ruthlessly dangerous. A fist grazed off her ribs and almost knocked her breath away. The eyes that approached her had murder in them, the hands that tore at her dress and twisted her flesh were animalistic and brutal. But their brutality was an even match for Dusty aroused to a blind rage and a hating defense of the last of her violated rights, and there was no room for fear. She had two steely fingers ruthlessly aimed at the closest eyes and one heel poised to kick and she was not beaten yet.

And then, suddenly, the odds were improved.

From nowhere a fourth man had appeared, he grabbed the nearest assailant and sent him spinning and crashing into the side of the truck. Taking advantage of the momentary disorientation caused by this turn of events, Dusty whirled and jammed her fist into the throat of the man behind her. He staggered back, gasping and choking, and from then on Dusty did not know what happened. They were fighting two against two, she felt the exhilaration of victory as she sensed fear in the opponents and the strength of her ally, and then suddenly, incredulously, truck doors were opening, an engine was roaring, men were swearing and shouting filthy threats, and gravel was flying beneath spinning truck tires.

With an instinctive roar of rage and despair Dusty lunged after them. They had her purse— her bag—all that she owned in the world! She had not fought like a hellion to be left stranded on the side of the road with even less than she had had before—with nothing, nothing at all! They were taking it all, she wouldn't let them take it all!

Strong hands were restraining her and she struggled wildly, screaming, "Let me go! They've got my purse. Let me go, you bastard!" With a sudden lunge of rage and residual barbarism Dusty whirled, bringing her foot up hard and ruthlessly. Once again, she missed, but the sharp heel that dug into his inner thigh was both unexpected and excruciatingly painful, and the brutal shove that was his automatic response sent her sprawling and sliding backward over the gravelly road shoulder, momentarily knocking her breath away.

When Dusty dizzily regained her bearings, the strange man was standing over her, bathed in the harsh headlights of what she now realized was an eighteen-wheeler drawn up behind them. His hands were clenched into fists and his face was drawn in anger and pain, he was breathing hard and regarding her incredulously. "Is *this* the way you thank me?" he exclaimed.

So this was her ally! This lean stranger in faded denims and rumpled checked shirt, lank blond hair falling over his forehead and a bristle of pale beard roughening his face—he didn't look much better than her assailants, and he had been a damn sight less helpful. She lay on the ground glaring up at him, and she spat furiously, "Thank you? Thank you for what?"

His face darkened with swiftly rising fury and his eyes sparked as he shot back, "For saving your cheap little hide for one thing! What the hell did you think you were doing—"

"You didn't save *anything*!" she screamed back at him. "I was doing fine until you came along with your idiotic Prince Valiant act—"

"You were outnumbered three to one! You're just a scrawny little girl—"

"And you're just a scrawny little boy! You let them take my purse! I could have stopped them but you let them get away! You *fool*! You didn't even *try* to go after them—"

"What the hell was I supposed to do, chase

them down on foot? I saved your life, damn it!"
he roared.

A sob of pure rage caught in Dusty's throat and
that was the last sound the night caught before it
dissolved into the ragged sound of their intermin-
gled breathing. They glared each other down, eyes
glittering and muscles taut. Dusty was too choked
with fury and defeat to speak, he was obviously
undergoing a great effort to regain control of the
temper that had been released by the unexpected
encounter with hoodlums and had only been
spurred by Dusty's irrational reception of his he-
roism. It was he who finally broke the eye contact,
the taut muscles of his arm visibly loosening
and fists uncurling as he released a long breath.
"Look," he said quietly, "I'm sorry I shoved you
and I'm sorry I yelled at you. I guess we're both still
wired, and you're getting a little hysterical—"

"I am not hysterical, you jackass," she snapped
at him, brushing away the hand he extended to
help her up, and scrambling to her feet unassisted.
His startled look swiftly turned to anger again as
she demanded, "Where's my other shoe?"

He cast one cold look around the circle of light
and walked two steps to retrieve the cast-off shoe,
growling, "These things should be registered as
deadly weapons. And just for the record,"—he
added coldly as he slapped the shoe into her out-
stretched hand—"this is the last time I ever risk
my life for a cheap trick in a tight dress, so maybe
you'd better go ply your trade on a safer street
corner."

"I am not a hooker!" she flared at him, and the way his cold disbelieving gaze raked over her partially exposed body twisted like a knife in her solar plexus, reminding her too well that that was the second time in twenty-four hours she had been taken for just that; reminding her with a stab of pain so sharp it actually took her breath away of all she had been running from, and for a moment she could say nothing else. All the fight drained out of her at once with the disgust in his eyes that traveled over her like probing fingers, and when he lifted his blank and utterly expressionless gaze to her face again she felt more naked and violated than she had in the hands of those boys. Dusty felt empty and exhausted and hurting and she simply wanted to find a place to crawl away and hide.

He said dully, "I don't really give a damn what you are. Get in the truck. I'm behind schedule."

He turned and walked in long rapid strides back toward the truck, and Dusty remained rooted to the spot. Was this it then, to escape from a gang rape only to walk straight into the arms of a man who thought even less of her than they had? She suddenly thought of her purse, the little canvas overnight bag that had contained all that remained of her life—three changes of clothes, two nightgowns, a toothbrush, and a make-up bag; the leather tooled wallet she had bought for herself one Christmas from a street vender, a paperback novel she had only half finished, a bottle of nail polish whose color she had not even tried yet, fifty dollars that did not exactly belong to her but was all the money she had in the world—and Dusty wanted to cry. Within the past twenty-four hours, she had endured heartbreak, humiliation, disillusionment, and the loss of a lifetime, but when she thought of her purse and her clothing in the dirty hands of those animals it was too much, and she just wanted to sink down onto the cold sand and sob until she couldn't cry any longer.

Midway to the truck, he turned, and called impatiently, "Well? Come on! I can't waste all night on you!"

Dusty whirled to face him, fists clenched and eyes glittering with unshed tears. "I'll thank you very kindly not to waste *any* more time on me!" she returned. "You've done quite enough already! Just get out of here and leave me alone!"

His incredulous, exasperated gaze was clear across the distance that separated them. "And just what the hell do you think you're going to do out here in the middle of the desert all by yourself?"

"I'm going to go to the nearest town and report this to the police!" she shouted furiously. "I'm going to get my things back!"

"The nearest town is two hundred miles away!" he jeered.

She was almost sobbing with frustration and renewed rage. "I don't care!" she screamed.

For just a moment he stood there and the anger that snapped between them was tight and palpable. Then with a furious flick of his wrist, he turned on his heel and strode to the truck.

"Walk!" he shouted back at her, and swung himself inside the cab.

She bent to slip on her sandal, and with a defiant toss of her head she straightened up and began her determined trek straight ahead. She refused to cry. She refused to do anything except let the empty, heavy pulse of her heart gradually meld into the slow roar of the engine. Behind her was pain and heartbreak and ahead of her were two hundred miles of empty highway but she wouldn't think about that. She wouldn't cry.

She had gone perhaps a hundred yards when the huge freighter pulled up beside her. The door opened and he moved back behind the steering column, looking down at her expressionlessly. She met his eyes for one long, calm moment, and then she gripped the handrailing to pull herself inside. He did not offer to assist, but merely waited until she pulled the heavy door closed behind her before he turned his attention to the gears, and his eyes to the road.

Chapter Two

Being inside the big truck was like being inside the cockpit of an airplane. It was so high off the ground that for a moment Dusty, who was not very good with heights anyway, actually felt dizzy. It was much roomier than she had expected, as big as a good-sized van inside, with room between the front seat and the dash for a large cooler and several pieces of accessorized equipment, a miniature television set and a tape storage rack. In the back was a space designated as living quarters, with a mattress covered in rumpled linen taking up most of the floor space, a rack for clothes, several large boxes whose contents were not very neatly arranged, even a small shelf for books and a worn guitar. The dash panel was lit with so many multicolored lights it looked like a computer console, and the interior smelled of travel and leather, stale beer, and old coffee grounds.

He glanced at her conversationally. "Ever been in one of these before?"

"Oh, sure," she lied negligently, curling her

legs up beneath her on the roomy seat. "Plenty of times."

The tight dress had ripped during the fight, and as she arranged her legs a length of thigh was exposed almost to the panty line. His eyes lingered for a moment on that smooth white flesh and she knew exactly what he was thinking—that she was the type of girl who spent a lot of time in big rigs, the backseats of cars, under doorways and behind bushes, anywhere she could. She didn't care. He wanted her to be a tramp, and she was not going to waste energy proving him wrong. She simply didn't care any longer.

He said smoothly, turning his eyes deliberately away from her leg and back to the road, "Lady, I've been on the road for six weeks and it's been longer than that since I've had a woman. Either fix that dress to cover what it's supposed to cover, or take it off completely and let's get it over with. But don't tease me, I don't think you'd like the consequences if you do."

For just a moment rebellion stirred and she glared at him defiantly. She had been pushed and shoved and treated like dirt once too often tonight and this seemed like the last straw. But something about the lean hard profile of his face called better judgment into play, and in the end it was the faintly stirring instinct for self-preservation that won out. Dusty put her feet back down on the floorboard, trying not to wince with every movement, and tugged the torn material of the dress, as well as she could, back into its original position.

It really was not worth fighting about. The same old story.

Dusty truly did not understand why she always seemed to have such a basic and perfectly predictable effect on men. She knew it was not true of all women. Other women could have men friends, other women could be respected and noticed for their abilities and their brains, not simply their bodies. Other women could hold powerful positions in the male world and sex would never enter into the picture. Other women, even beautiful ones, could walk across the room and receive no more than respectful, admiring glances, and sometimes they were not even noticed at all. Dusty was not beautiful, but she was always noticed.

Her face was small and square, her jaw line unattractively stubborn, her nose straight and unremarkable. Her lips were full, but because they were usually drawn into grim lines, they were not a seductive feature. Her eyes were a dark blue that sometimes looked murky gray, they were not beautifully shaped, or widely spaced, and very rarely held sensual allure. Mostly her eyes were hard, sometimes defensive, always a window to the quick intelligence and calculating mind that worked behind them. Her chestnut hair was thick and wavy, shorn at the collar line and curling inward over her neck, heavy on top with a tendency to shadow her eyes. It was glossy and bouncy, reflecting the healthy glow of a fine young animal, the type of hair a man would like to run his fingers through and capture by the handful. But to Dusty it was just hair. Besides, men rarely looked at her hair, or her face, or her eyes. When Dusty passed, the male gaze was usually directed much lower.

Dusty had a perfect figure. She did not know why, or how, she never worked at it and she certainly considered it more of a curse than a blessing, but it was something she simply was born with, and no matter how hard Dusty dieted or gorged herself, her measurements remained the same. Hips and bust a perfect thirty-six, waist a trim and unrelenting twenty-four. On a taller girl this might have passed unremarked, or even have been considered only for its aesthetic attributes, but Dusty was small, every man's dream of the perfect toy doll, and the word "sexpot" had never been more appropriately used to describe a woman's appearance. Dusty hated it, but there was nothing she could do about it. She was used to the fact that when she spoke to a man his gaze never moved above her neck, she was used to overhearing comments like, "A lot of sex in a little package," and, "More than a handful is twice as good." But she never learned to like it.

Tonight she knew she looked like every man's fantasy—or at least she had, before the fight. Tonight, heavily made up and dressed in the ridiculous sheath and spiked heels she looked like everything she hated and everything Peter lusted after; she looked like a high-priced hooker which was, of course, exactly the effect Peter had been striving for. Dusty was more comfortable in loose jeans and sloppy sweatshirts than evening clothes, and at work she disguised her feminine attributes with modest skirts and prim blouses. Even that did not help. It was as though she exuded some sort of primitive sexuality of which she was not even aware but which the male animal could sniff out inexorably, as though there were some sort of body chemistry that seeped from her pores and triggered male hormones with unfailing accuracy, and there was absolutely nothing she could do to stop it. Dusty knew that if she had cared to capitalize on her advantage she could have had anything she wanted from any man who crossed her path, but she had never, ever, used sex as a bartering power. And she never would. That was what the men simply couldn't understand, and that was why she had spent all of her life fighting so hard and gaining so little.

The reminder of her most recent loss was like another physical blow to her already battered body and the lump that filled her throat almost choked her. She had to swallow twice, hard, and clench her fists against the urge to simply curl up into a little ball and cry. She said harshly, "So what are you going to do about getting my purse back, hotshot?"

There was a slight tightening of his lips and he worked the last three gears with a rough energy. He was not a very large man, just under six feet and slimly built, but the muscles of his arms were tight and well developed, rippling with the strength that came from keeping the big machine under control day after day. For just a moment Dusty watched, in fascination, the movement of those bunched muscles beneath the light fabric of his shirt, and then he said with commendable control of tone, "I'm not going back to Vegas. I can call in a police report over the CB and you can fill out the papers when we get to the next town. That's the best I can do."

"Did you get the licence number?" she challenged him.

He was silent, and she scoffed recklessly, "Oh, the big bad hero!" Her throat was aching from the effort not to cry and her nails dug into her palms. "You came sailing up on your white charger and screwed everything all to hell!"

"You've got a garbage mouth, lady," he returned shortly. His voice was calm but she could see the tightening of his muscles through his shirt. "You keep it up and you might just wish I'd left you back there with those boys."

She twisted in the seat to look at him, her eyes flaring with near-hysteria as the accumulated pain— emotional and physical—began to take its toll. "I would have been better off!" she lashed back. "It might have escaped your notice, but I'd been doing pretty well for myself before you came along! Did you happen to notice? Did you? I was doing just fine until Mr. Tough Guy burst on the scene and scared them off. Another two minutes and I would have at least had my purse back! But no, you had to *help*!"

She saw with faint satisfaction the tightening of

the muscle of his jaw and a dull flush tinge his shadowed face, and she knew she had made her point. He could not deny that three would-be assailants had suffered more from their tussle with her than from him, and in all likelihood she would have managed just fine without his interference. It did not occur to her that she had threatened his virility by pointing out that she was better in a street fight than he was, nor did she care. She only knew that she had scored a small knife thrust for the many that had been inflicted upon her today and the pleasure she felt in the fact was vicious. He reached forward and jerked the CB mike off the stand, saying stiffly, "Do you want me to report it or not?"

The small satisfaction Dusty had felt in her victory drained away into emptiness, leaving only the throbbing ache of body and spirit. What good would it do? Who cared that she had lost everything she owned, a few meager cosmetics, bargain basement clothing, and a tooled leather wallet that had been a Christmas gift to herself? Who cared about Dusty Macleod except Dusty Macleod? "No," she said at last, tiredly, leaning her head back. "I'll never get it back. There's no point."

He glanced at her as he replaced the microphone, leaving the interior of the truck to the static hum of faraway voices and the muted roar of wheels on the pavement. Dusty might have been touched by the softening sympathy that crossed his face with that glance, or she might have been angered, but at any rate she did not see it. Her eyes were fixed blankly on the wide black stretch of highway ahead, the unbounded bleak night that seemed to breed and multiply as the slice of the truck's headlights ate up mile after mile of it. The unadorned emptiness that stretched before them was a reflection of her life—just forever, as far as the eye could see, nothing.

His voice was gruff as he inquired after a moment, "So what did you have in that purse, anyway? Your life savings?"

The short laugh she gave could have easily turned into a sob. She was hurting all over and the longer she sat there the more acutely aware she became of the fact. Her feet were like twin flames, pulsing and throbbing from the bone outward, and the muscles in her legs ached so badly she could not make the slightest movement without biting her lip against the pain. She could not believe she had walked that far. Even her stomach muscles hurt and the shoulder that had taken the weight of her bag was raw and stiff. She could feel a swelling bruise on her rib cage where the fist had landed and rough handprints battered her arms and her chest and even her hips. Her head ached with exhaustion and tension. She was tired of playing it tough and she only wanted to be left alone.

"Yeah," she replied dryly, "you could say that." With an excruciating effort she bent to slip the sandals from her feet. They were sticky and gritty with sand and the pain that sliced though her as she moved the shoes over open blisters brought tears to her eyes. But there was no sign of personal agony in her face as she straightened up and added coolly, "Fifty dollars, to be exact, that I stole from a hotel room in Vegas."

She watched him carefully for a reaction, not bothering to wonder why she was going to so much trouble to make certain he thought the worst of her. But he only said, slipping a tape into the deck and turning up the volume, "Are the police after you?"

She made another small sound of derision and leaned back. "Hardly." The Eagles played background rhythm for the sound of the tires on the empty highway, and she closed her eyes wearily, feeling sick and defeated. It was useless to wonder how she got here, a thousand miles from nowhere, victim of the dubious mercies of a man she did not know, with the future stretching like a blank canvas before her and the past an abyss at her back. There was too much pain in looking back and nothing to look toward, and all she wanted to do was cry.

Her sharply honed sixth sense told her that he was looking at her, and when she opened her eyes suspiciously she was surprised by something almost like concern on his face. He said, "Are you all right? Did they hurt you?"

She sat up straight, careful not to grimace with the movement, and replied stiffly, "No. I'm not hurt."

There was impatience in his movement as he looked back to the road, but it was another moment before he spoke. "What the hell were you doing out there in the middle of nowhere, anyway?" he demanded, for some reason angry again. "Just where did you think you were going?"

She was too tired to fight any longer. She simply told the truth, in a dull, rather drained voice. "I didn't realize how far it was between towns out here. I'm from the East."

"No kidding?" His voice was mocking. "Just what part of the Bronx are you from, anyway?" That drew a small glare from her, and apparently satisfied, he explained in a more equitable tone, "Your accent is so thick you could cut it with a knife."

She looked uncomfortably out the window. "Only when I'm tired—or mad," she replied, not knowing why she bothered to answer him at all.

He leaned forward and took two beers from the cooler at her feet, passing one to her before straightening up again. She murmured a surprised, though somewhat disgruntled, "Thanks" and opened it. She couldn't remember when she had eaten last—time was meaningless in the City of Lights—but beer was better than nothing. She doubted whether she could choke down anything more solid anyway.

He supported the can between his thighs as he pulled the tab, and his tone was almost pleasant as he inquired, "What's your name?"

"Dusty," she answered automatically. "Dusty Macleod."

Amusement twitched his lips as he glanced at her. "Where'd you get a name like that?"

She shrugged tiredly. "I don't know. I think my grandmother named me. She was weird."

"It's a boy's name, isn't it? Short for Dustin?"

"Maybe," she replied disinterestedly. "It's Dusty on my birth certificate, though."

He was silent for a time, sipping his beer, and the music filled up the space between them. Dusty grew drowsy beneath the hypnotic sway of the road and the effects of the alcohol on an empty stomach, but after a while she roused herself enough to inquire, "Where are you headed?"

"Santa Fe, this trip." He glanced at her briefly. "We should be hitting civilization by daylight. I can let you off at the first town, or I'll be stopping in Flagstaff tomorrow night."

She shrugged dispiritedly. "Doesn't matter." Nothing did anymore. She would be no better off in Flagstaff than she would be in Denver or Phoenix or Austin or even New York. But she was simply too tired, too beaten and aching and bone weary to worry about it tonight. She leaned her head back and closed her eyes, letting the draining lethargy creep over her. Too tired to fight any longer, she fell asleep with the half-empty can of beer clutched in her hands.

She awoke with a jerk, whirling wildly and swinging automatically, when she felt a hand on her knee. She caught a glimpse of his startled face before the hand that had been on her knee came up in instinctive defense and knocked her arm back, hard and ruthless, before it could strike his face. "You little hellcat!" He whipped his attention back to the road but not before she got a glimpse of the glittering slits of his eyes and the dark rage that suffused his face. She was still blurry with sleep and disoriented, every muscle of her body screaming protest at the abrupt awakening and the sudden movement, and she did not notice the brief and violent battle he fought to bring the truck back under control. "Do you want to get us both killed? Don't you ever try anything like that again!"

"Keep your hands off me!" she screamed back, shaking with animal instinct and throbbing pain, too confused and disoriented to wonder why he should be upset.

"I've got my hands full with a machine that's a hell of a lot more valuable than you are," he shot back, breathing hard. The hands that gripped the steering wheel were white-knuckled. "When I want to sneak a feel you can be damned sure I won't risk my rig for it." He took a short breath that was a visible effort to bring his temper back under control, and Dusty was even more confused as she gradually realized that there had been a moment of real danger, and that he was blaming her for it. Then he said tersely, not looking at her, "You won't be able to move in a few hours if you try to sleep sitting up. Go in back and lie down."

She stared at him, gradually understanding. He had only been trying to wake her up and her over-reaction had almost caused an accident—no wonder he was angry! "I—I'm sorry..." she stammered.

"Just get out of my sight," he snapped, his eyes on the road, and Dusty stiffly got up to do as she was told.

The mattress was wonderfully soft, enveloping her aching body like a cloud. The cool sheets smelled male, the pillow bore the indentation of his head. She wanted to think about him, wondering why he had stopped to help her, why he was bothering with her now, what kind of man he was and what fate awaited her at his hands, but she couldn't make her fuzzy mind focus. She was asleep again almost before she closed her eyes.

Chapter Three

Some subconscious awareness must have told her that the truck had stopped moving. A pink-gray dawn filtered through her half-opened eyes and she turned and stretched automatically.

The pain that clenched and twisted in her leg was so sharp and agonizing that she couldn't help crying out. She sat up straight and tried to massage it with stiff fingers, a sob breaking through as the agony only tightened and redoubled.

He was beside her in a moment, his face grim as he demanded, "Cramp?"

She nodded, biting her lip hard against a sob as the twisting muscles knotted all the way from her calf to her thigh in a pain that was as excruciating as any she had ever known. His strong hard fingers took over the task hers had started and then she did sob, trying to push the probing, hurting hands away. But he ignored her, and his voice was soothing as he said, "I know. But it'll ease up in a minute. Give it a chance."

She knew he was right and she sank back

against the mattress, clenching her teeth and squeezing her eyes shut as his deft, competent hands worked the knotted muscles, intensifying the pain at first and then, gradually, easing it. Heedlessly he brushed away the torn material over her thigh and impersonally worked the hard muscle there until he felt it begin to relax beneath his fingers. The worst of the pain subsided and she self-consciously began to rearrange the material of her dress, murmuring shakily, "Thanks— it's better."

He moved his hands away, but he did not get up. She felt him looking at her and all her defensive instincts rose to the surface when she heard his short, soft intake of breath. This was it then, the time he expected her to pay for her ride, for why else would he have stopped the truck? Anger boiled and her old spirit kindled. She may be down but she was not out and she would be damned if she would lie here like a sacrificial virgin and let him take what he thought was his due....

She sat up quickly, ready to fight and disregarding the fact that, in her present condition, any resistance she could put up would be only token. The very act of sitting up was an exercise in agony. But then she was surprised and disoriented to find that he was not looking at her legs, or her abdomen, or her breasts, but at her feet. And he said, softly, "My God! What did you do to yourself?"

She followed his gaze in some confusion to her bare feet. They looked as bad as they felt. Swollen and blistered, torn and caked with dirt and dried blood, they were not a very pretty sight at all. There was incredulity in his face and anger underscored his tone as he looked back at her. "Did you *walk* all the way from Las Vegas?" he demanded—and why that concept seemed to upset him so Dusty could not imagine.

"How else do you think I got to the desert?" she returned somewhat acerbically, irritated with him because he was irritated with her, and she did not know why.

His eyes widened with a mixture of emotions, not the least of which was a very irrational anger. "You *walked*—in those—those..." He gestured futilely toward the front seat where her shoes still lay. When he looked back at her his eyes were churning. That was the first time that Dusty noticed he had blue eyes, like her own, but now they looked closer to black. "You little idiot!" he exploded at her. "Do you have any idea how far that was? Do you realize what could have happened to you? What the *hell* were you thinking about?"

Dusty winced at his onslaught, as confused as she was angered by it. "I don't want to know how far it was," she shot back hotly. "It's none of your business, anyway! Just get off my case, will you?"

He gave her one murderous look and then stood abruptly, swinging out of the cab with an ugly oath. "Stay put," he snapped over his shoulder, and walked away.

Dusty had no intention of doing anything else. She sank back wearily on her elbows, subduing nausea and trying not to groan with the pain that still invaded her leg muscles. She could see from the window that they had pulled into a rest stop, but it was empty except for them. The sky was a pearly pink-gray, barely dawn, the world around her unearthly still except for the pulsing throb of the incessant engine.

She heard his footsteps on the asphalt outside and she sat up, ready to do battle again. But when he knelt beside her she saw that he had a basin of water in his hands, and his only words were a commmand for her to put her feet in it.

He watched her carefully as she gingerly obeyed, as though expecting her to cry out. There was an amused flicker of admiration in his eyes when she determinedly did not. The warm water stung like acid, and she had to keep her lips tightly compressed. He rummaged around for a washcloth and found a bar of soap, and his back was to her as he asked in a peculiar tone, "What were you running away from?"

She was afraid if she didn't answer he would guess, quite correctly, that it was because she was in too much pain to reply. She said stiffly, "A man." That was all she could manage, and more than he had a right to know.

The look in his eyes was very strange, gentle, probing, worriedly curious, and she dropped her own gaze in confusion beneath it. He said no more, but his hands were very gentle as he bathed her feet and blotted them dry, then applied a soothing ointment from the first-aid kit and wrapped them in gauze. At first she had flinched whenever he touched her, but by the time he was finished she had learned to relax beneath his ministrations. She was surprised at the tenderness and care he was capable of exercising, and at his sensitivity to every slight indication she made of pain. She would not have believed that his hands, so rough and calloused and filled with sinewy strength, could be so soft when they touched her, so delicate when they tended her. She was amazed to sense something within her begin to change and soften in response to him, and it was an alien feeling . . . something almost like trust.

She did not like that feeling, for it seemed to make her entirely too vulnerable. She was careful to keep her face blank as she gave him an impersonal, "Thanks." But she did not go so far as to remind him that she could have done it all herself. Not this time.

He turned to put away the first-aid kit, replying, "Stay off them today and you'll probably be all right. I don't want to waste more time at the emergency room of some county hospital."

But she was already standing, and when he turned there was astonishment and annoyance on his face. "Where the hell do you think you're going? I told you—"

"To the bathroom?" she requested sweetly. "That is, if it won't put you too much more behind schedule"

With a scowl and a curse he stood and, in a single movement, lifted her into his arms. She could only gasp, "What are you doing? You can't—"

"I can and I will," he replied grimly, springing to the ground with her in his arms with the agility of a dancer. She would not have thought he was that strong, but he carried her as though her weight were nothing to him. "I don't have time to fool with an infection, not after all the trouble I've just gone to to get you cleaned up."

She glanced around anxiously as he carried her with long easy strides across the asphalt and the stretch of cactus-strewn sand toward the restrooms, but still they were alone. When he pushed open the door of the ladies' room with one shoulder she gasped again, in real consternation, "You can't go in there!"

He gave her a look of amused forebearance and replied, "If anyone objects, we'll just tell them you're my mother and I'm afraid to go to the bathroom by myself."

He sat her down carefully on the tiled floor and looked as though he had every intention of staying and waiting for her. She was embarrassed, and she could not remember the last time she had been embarrassed. Why should this màn have the power to embarrass her when she had, in her short lifetime, been abused by experts and never shown any ill-effects? For the first time since their meeting her scathing wit and quick tongue deserted her, and she could only look at him in mute appeal.

Perhaps the dignity of her silence touched him, for if it had been his intention to carry out this final humiliation he apparently changed his mind. There was a moment of hesitation, and then he looked uncomfortable. "Two minutes," he said gruffly, turning towards the door. "Don't come outside; I'll come back for you."

He did not even allow her time to wash her face of the streaked and matted make-up, or make even a cursory inspection of her appearance in the mirror. He carried her back to the truck without a word and placed her on the mattress. They were rolling again before she even thought to thank him, or wondered if she should.

When next she woke it was to the sounds of an Eddie Rabbit cassette and the morning sun in her eyes. This time she stretched gingerly, grimacing more from the fuzzy taste in her mouth and the empty rumbling of her stomach than from muscular pain. She lay there for a moment, looking around her, trying to get used to the uncertainties this day might hold. In her direct line of vision was a row of shirts hanging neatly on the rack, and some jeans folded over hangers. Below that was a box containing more clothes, folded T-shirts on top, and a heavy alpaca jacket. There were a couple of pairs of cowboy boots, some sneakers, and miscellaneous toiletries belonging to a man. But it was the shelf of books that fascinated her, and she glanced at the back of his neck curiously. He had not struck her as the type of man who liked to read. Interspersed among dog-eared paperback novels were some very high-brow volumes—history, politics, art, Plato's *Republic* and other classics, even a couple in foreign languages she could not read. Some of them looked like college textbooks. She frowned curiously and glanced at him again, but she did not spend much time trying to figure him out. By the end of the day they would have parted ways, and then...

And then... she tried not to sigh out loud as she turned over on her back and stared blankly up at the roof of the vehicle. She thought in bland despair, *How did it ever get this crazy?*

"There are some sandwich fixings in that cooler beside you." He raised his voice over the country-rock rhythm of twanging guitars. "Make me one too, will you?"

She sat up, scowling at him. "What am I, your personal slave or something?"

"There's no such thing as a free ride, baby," he replied cheerfully over his shoulder, and her frown only deepened as she wondered just how much she would be expected to pay for this one.

She knew she should be ashamed of herself for rebelling over such a little thing as fixing him a sandwich, but she wasn't. She knew she would still be stranded on a Nevada highway right now, probably slowly dying of exposure, if it weren't for him, and for that she supposed she should be grateful. He had been kind to her this morning and he hadn't needed to be. But in the end the only reason she turned grudgingly to the cooler was because she was starving, and her own sense of fair play would not let her eat his food and refuse to share.

There was bologna and cheese, and small jars of mayonnaise and mustard, and white bread. The very thought of a bologna sandwich for breakfast turned her stomach, but she supposed she had done worse. She made two sandwiches and passed his to him without a word. He accepted it in like manner.

She sat cross-legged on the mattress behind him and hungrily consumed half the sandwich without tasting it. The edge of her appetite now dulled, she finished the rest more slowly, finding it harder and harder to eat as the cold knowledge of her predicament formed a hard knot around the contents of her stomach. She could see out the front window miles and miles of stretching highway flanked by dull and barren desert, differing only from the night view in that it was all much clearer now. Just as the few hours' sleep had cleared her own brain, the daylight cast no shadows over harsh and irrefutable realities. She was alone again. Abandoned in the middle of nowhere, penniless, friendless, with nothing to fall back on and nowhere to go. She tried not to be afraid.

"You make a sloppy sandwich, kid," he said, and extended his mustard-smeared hand backward over the seat to her.

She glared at him, starting to demand what he expected her to do about it, but he answered that question for her with surprising good humor, "A paper towel will do just fine. There's a roll back there somewhere."

She found the paper towels, tore one off, and slapped it into his hand ungraciously. She forced down the last bit of her own sandwich and then demanded, "What do we get to wash this stuff down with? Beer?"

He leaned forward and took a single-serving can of orange juice from the cooler, passing it over the seat to her. But when she pulled the pop tab he said, "Thanks, darlin'," and took it from her again.

For another moment she bored murderous daggers into the back of his shaggy-blond head, and then she got up and climbed ungracefully over the seat to plop down beside the passenger door. She rummaged through the cooler until she found another can of orange juice and drank it thirstily, never once looking at him.

And then she said suddenly, "Where are my shoes?"

The front of the rig, unlike the back, was kept spotlessly clean, unlittered and faultlessly organized. There was nothing on the floorboard beneath her feet and she distinctly remembered leaving her shoes there last night.

He replied implacably, "I threw them out."

The shock, the fury, the exploding pain that assailed her, was totally inappropriate. But it was so overwhelming that it took her breath away and all she could do was stare at him, the one word she could manage was a choked, "Why?"

Unconsciously he rubbed his inner thigh where she had kicked him, answering, "Aside from the fact that you should have a license to carry them"—he glanced at her easily—"they were no good to you any more. You certainly couldn't wear them with your feet in the shape they're in, and if you tried you'd probably cripple yourself."

"But they were all I had!" she cried. Her eyes were dark and her white cheeks suddenly flooded with violent color. The red rage that swept her blotted out everything else, and the only thing that mattered was the sound of her hoarse, wild, furious voice that was choked and torn with yet another violation of her fragile personal rights. Just as the loss of her purse last night had borne the weight of the loss of her dreams, so now did his callous disposal of her shoes seem to symbolize the way her entire life had been ripped away by others without her consent. Her eyes glittered and her lips were white as she twisted toward him, ready to lunge. "You lousy, filthy—you had no right! They were mine! You arrogant son of a bitch. How *dare* you!"

"Dammit, lady, I warned you!" His hand shot out to ward her off, his former good humor vanishing in an instant into quick anger and lightning reflexes as he divided his attention between keeping her away from him and keeping the truck on the road. "Stay the hell away from me when I'm driving!" When she struggled, breathing hard and hungry for blood, his hand captured her wrist in a bone crushing grip, drawing a startled sound of pain from her.

"What will you do next?" she screamed at

him, completely beyond rationality now. "Strip me naked and leave me by the side of the road?"

"Don't tempt me!" he spat back viciously, and in an abrupt, snapping movement, he braced the hand that still twisted her wrist against her chest and shoved her hard. He did not take his eyes off the road as she bounced against the door.

The sound that was wrenched from her could have been a sob, but she would not give him the satisfaction of knowing so. Still shaking and almost incoherent with shock and rage, she called him every vile gutter name she had ever heard and even invented a few for the occasion, and was satisfied to see his eyes widen and the anger drain from his face into a look of astonishment, as though it shocked him that a woman—any woman—would know such words, much less actually speak them. His reaction might have been amusing under normal circumstances, but Dusty was far beyond being amused by anything. When she broke off, breathless and spent, there was utter silence for the span of about five seconds.

The calm tone of his voice was surprising, inappropriate, and completely disorienting. It had an abrupt draining affect on Dusty. He said simply, "Is that all?"

Suddenly she was too tired to even move. She searched for the anger, the indignation, the sense of desecration, and could find none of it. He had taken everything from her, even her anger, and she did not even have the emotion left to cry about it. Her eyes were resting on the lean brown hand that guided the steering wheel, her ears were filled with CB static and the lonesome whine of tires, and it just didn't matter any more. Nothing did.

He was waiting for a reply, so she said dully, somewhat hoarsely, "Yes."

"Good." His voice, like his face in profile, was completely expressionless. "Because if I ever hear language like that from you again I'm going to wash your mouth out with soap—it's an old-fashioned remedy but it never fails, and I guess you know I'd do it, too, don't you?"

She looked at that lean hard profile, the exterior calm that subdued an inner storm, and she had no doubt that he would. Some deeply ingrained instinct warned her never to take any threat this man made lightly. She had seen his gentleness and she had seen his violence and she knew much more lay beneath the surface that she might be better off never seeing.

He turned very bright, utterly blank blue eyes upon her, demanding an answer, and a sudden urgency warned her not to push him any further. She answered slowly, "Yes," and looked away. Apparently satisfied, he turned his own attention back to the road.

Very faintly, a sense of the ludicrousness of the entire situation stirred. After all she had been through, she had wanted to kill him over a pair of shoes. And overriding his tolerance and generosity to her the past twenty-four hours, the only thing he had found intolerable was her offensive language. That was especially absurd when she remembered a few words he had uttered last night during the fight and again this morning when he had been so upset by the condition of her feet, words that were not exactly dictionary standard. Somehow, very vaguely, that made her almost want to smile.

He put another tape in the player and Willie Nelson was crooning his ballads. Miles passed, and then he said, his tone subdued, "I'll buy you another pair of shoes."

She made no reply. She simply stared out the window and tried not to wonder what good shoes would do her when she had no place to go.

After another long time filled with Willie's twangy ballads and the dull hum of the engine, he said quietly, "Look, I know you've had a rough time and I guess you have a right to be touchy. But we've six hours to go before Flagstaff and I'm willing to call a truce if you are. Let's try to get along."

"Miles to go before I sleep," murmured Dusty absently, and she looked up just in time to catch his startled look. "I do know some words that aren't censored," she explained wryly, and his slow, soft smile was unexpectedly gratifying. She had to look away quickly because that smile was also touching—in the sense that it seemed briefly to reach through her defenses and urge a response from her. It made her want to relax her guard and share the moment, it made her feel vulnerable.

She spoke abruptly, a sign that she was willing to accept the truce but no more, and her words were impersonal, almost cold. "What's your name?"

He seemed to hesitate before answering, his lips twitched with mirth as he anticipated her reaction to his answer. "Camp," he said.

"Camp?" She lifted a dryly amused eyebrow. "First or last name?"

"Both."

She muttered under her breath, "And you made fun of *my* name."

He chuckled. "So we're even," he said, all of his former good humor now apparently restored.

Reluctantly, almost grudgingly, a tight smile tugged at the corners of her lips, and he caught it out of the corner of his eye. "Nice," he said. "That's the first time I've seen you smile."

She looked away, feeling the tension and the despair begin to slowly creep back into her limbs again. "There hasn't been too much to smile about lately." It was not a plea for sympathy, just a simple statement of fact, and he accepted it as such. He offered no meaningless platitudes, or understanding looks—not that she would have expected either sympathy or understanding from him anyway—and she was somehow grateful for that.

Camp retrieved from somewhere around his seat two apples, one of which he tossed to her. At her uncertain glance he explained, "Good for the digestion," and bit into the apple. After a moment she followed suit, hoping the fruit would calm her queasy stomach and, as an after-effect, soothe her anxious nerves.

She inquired in a moment, "Is this rig yours?"

"Ten per cent mine," he replied cheerfully, "forty per cent the bank's, and fifty per cent the mortgage company's. In other words I'm in hock up to my—" He broke off with a grin and a sideways glance at her to which she could not help but respond. "Sorry. I guess if I'm going to clean up your language the first place I'd better start is with my own."

She shrugged, taking another bite of the apple. It was fresh and crisp and exactly what her uneasy stomach needed after the assault made upon it by breakfast. "Don't strain yourself. I know how truckers talk. And I guess you've already figured out that nothing you can say will shock me."

"The English language is a magnificent tool," he replied seriously. "It shouldn't be abused by anyone; especially," he added with a glance at her, "by ladies."

Her sharp bark of laughter was both in astonishment at his old-fashioned idea of chivalry and a defense against the fact that that was the first time anyone had ever referred to her as a lady and meant it. That touched her. She did not want to analyze why, but it did. "Thank you, Professor Higgins!" she retorted, and then, in a mimicked cockney accent, "I'll do me best to please, sir!"

Again he grinned, and spared a few seconds from the road to look at her. She was taken aback first by the friendly, open warmth in his suncrinkled eyes, and then by the fact that he was actually looking at her face ... not at her partially exposed bosom or the curve of her lap or the swell of her thigh, but at her eyes, and her smile. He was looking at her as one person would look at another, and what he saw seemed to bring him pleasure. He looked at her and his eyes softened, and with that softening something deep inside her stirred that was unsettling and completely unfamiliar to her . . . but nice. She had to quickly look away, disoriented and confused but, just for a brief moment, pleased.

Camp leaned back against the seat, one hand easily guiding the steering wheel, finishing off the apple with relaxed leisure. After a time Dusty looked back at him, really looking at him for the first time.

He was hardly any woman's ideal of Prince Charming. She guessed he wasn't much older than she was, in his late twenties, perhaps, though the rough stubble of unattractive blond beard made it difficult to tell much of anything about his face. His hair could have used a good cut and style, although it probably would look better after shampooing. Now it was straight and wiry, dirty blond layers falling haphazardly whichever way his fingers happened to guide them. The wrinkled blue checked shirt was stained with perspiration and the tight, often-bleached jeans were marked with streaks of oil and mud. His eyes were hollow-shadowed and bloodshot, and the puffiness of fatigue exaggerated his cheekbones. He looked dead on his feet, but from his unusually buoyant mood she suspected he had taken some of those infamous pep pills truck drivers always kept on hand. Dusty wondered how long he had been driving before he had stopped for her.

"Do you always drive straight through like this," she inquired worriedly, "without stopping to sleep?"

"No," he replied cheerfully, tossing the apple core into a litter bag on the console. "Sometimes I fall asleep at the wheel." At her skeptical glance he assured her, "It's true. I once crossed a whole state sound asleep. Fortunately," he added philosophically, turning his eyes back to the road, "it was a small state."

She smothered a laugh by quickly taking another bite out of the apple, but his eyes were twinkling when he glanced at her. "So, Dusty," he said pleasantly, "if you're not a hooker, what are you?"

"An accountant," she replied immediately, and she tried very hard not to be irritated by the disbelief he attempted to hide by turning his eyes quickly back to the road. "A damn good one, too," she defended harshly, tossing the apple beside his in the litter bag. She waited for him to challenge her, her eyes wary and her fists clenching unconsciously, but he obviously was not going to fight with her again today.

"Nice work," he commented mildly, "if you can do it. Myself, I can't add two and two without coming up with five and a half."

"Which is probably," she pointed out, relieved, "why you're in hock up to your..." Her lips tightened against a smile as she finished politely, "Ears."

Camp flashed her another endearing, amused grin, and she felt everything inside her begin to soften and relax in response to him. "Could be," he agreed cheerfully. "Where's home to you, Dusty?"

And all the warm pleasure that had begun to fill her veins was drained away with that question and replaced with cold emptiness. She looked back out the window toward the ceaseless, monotonous highway and simply shrugged. She didn't trust her voice for anything else.

She could feel the curiousity in his eyes, and the gentle disbelief in his voice made her want to tell him to mind his own business. She restrained herself. "No family?" he prompted. "No friends? No job to go back to?"

"No," she answered tonelessly, wishing immediately she had had the foresight, or the energy, to lie to him. The truth would only prolong a discussion of a subject she was trying very hard to avoid thinking about right now.

Sensing her mood, he was silent for a time. But then he had to ask, with genuine interest behind the quietness of his tone, "What are your plans?"

She lifted her head, as though that very gesture could defy the demons of emptiness, and replied negligently, "I'll get by. I always do."

If he noticed a quaver in the firm confidence of her tone he did not give any indication of it. Camp put another tape in the deck and this time it was Glen Campbell. After a time of nothing but the mournful tale of the girl he left behind and the flat desert highway stretching endlessly before them, Dusty straightened up and, with a breath, tried to recapture the easy rapport that had been between them before. She said pleasantly, "What about you? Where is home?"

He made a circular motion with his wrist. "This is it," he replied easily. "A post office box and my rig."

She frowned a little in puzzlement. The concept of home, of roots, of a place and possessions she could call her own, was too important to her for her to be able to easily understand anyone who could be so casual about the absence of such things. "Do you like it that way?" she inquired.

He shrugged. "It's not a question of liking it, that's just the way it is. I'm on the road three hundred days a year if I'm lucky, and keeping a place is a luxury I can't afford." And then Camp added, almost to himself, "It does get lonely sometimes."

But something had come over his face with that last remark, a bleakness, almost, and though he did not look at her she could tell her question had opened doors on things he, too, preferred not to think about. She did not know what to say to him then, and the emptiness and the distance that stretched before them were mirrored inside the truck between them.

Dusty sat back and closed her eyes, too tired

now to fight the anxieties and the uncertainties that must be faced. He had said Flagstaff tonight. What was in Flagstaff? What was anywhere for a girl in a tattered cocktail dress with no shoes and no money and not even a friend to turn to? Those she had left behind in New York would not even remember her name. Dusty had never made friends easily, and she rarely stayed in one place long enough to try. The only person she had ever really been close to was Peter, and he...

She clenched her teeth against the unplanned flood of hot tears that gorged her throat and refused to look back. There was always the Salvation Army. It wasn't a very comforting thought, but it was the best she could do. After all, forever stretched ahead of her and she had to start somewhere.

Dusty drifted off into an uneasy sleep to the litany of, *Something will work out. It just has to....*

And the wheels rolled on.

Chapter Four

They hit the Flagstaff City Limits late in the afternoon, and by that time Dusty was more than grateful for the journey's end. Somehow the easy companionship that had almost gotten started between them never completely resumed—either that, or the pills he had taken had begun to wear off shortly after their conversation that morning.

When Dusty awoke after a fretful hour's sleep Camp did not make an attempt to engage in anything other than perfunctory conversation and Dusty did not have the energy to try to draw him out. He stopped once for refueling, but even that was done rapidly, methodically, and he never mentioned lunch. The rest of the afternoon was spent to the incessant beat of country rock and the nauseating sway of the truck, and Dusty was so bored and travel-weary every nerve in her body felt on the verge of screaming. For a while the traffic on the well-traveled expressway provided some distraction, but even that grew old after a while. Talking to him would have been a welcome relief, but he looked so worn and weary she knew anything she might say to him would only put her in danger of another fight. By the time he signaled his exit from the freeway she was certain she would never want to get in another moving vehicle again, and if she had to listen to one more whining ballad about the joys and tribulations of life on the road, she would surely scream.

Just outside the exit, as Camp pulled into the large well-occupied truck stop, Dusty could sense his spirits rise—a renewal of energy—even as hers conversely began to sink. It was a reaction she should have been prepared for, she knew, but somehow she wasn't. This was it. There was no more time to postpone worry and avoid the future because this was it, the end of the line, this was where she got off. She had not realized before how much simply being with him had shielded her from the realities she must face, and now that she was on her own again the despair that filled her was almost overwhelming.

Camp parked the truck carefully, turned off the motor, and then leaned back against the seat with a long and satisfied sigh. "A hot shower and a square meal," he murmured with visible self-indulgent anticipation. "I've forgotten what either one of them feels like."

With renewed enthusiasm he stretched over the seat to retrieve his duffle bag, and it wasn't until he had opened the door and started to alight that he looked back at her. A faint frown puckered his brow, as though he had only that moment remembered her presence and the problems it created. Obviously, he wasn't used to worrying about anyone but himself.

But he did not let that trouble him for more than a moment, and in no way permitted present problems to detract from his pleasure at having made his goal. "Why don't you get cleaned up, too," he suggested, "and we'll have something to eat. You can slip on a pair of my sneakers for the time being, but don't go walking around too much on those feet." He sprang lightly to the ground and then turned back, another very faint frown troubling his features as his gaze swept back over her. "And don't go loitering around the showers," he warned, his eyes for just a moment lingering with disturbing accuracy over the swell of her bosom and the curve of naked thigh visible through the torn material. "Some pretty rough characters hang out around here. Just get your business done and come back to the truck. I'll meet you here."

Another time she would have laughed at the vision of herself trying to pick up men outside a ladies' shower dressed in a torn cocktail dress and a pair of men's sneakers. But now it didn't seem funny. Now it didn't seem as though anything would ever be funny again. Something about his casual dismissal of her—another inconvenience neatly taken care of—triggered a breakdown of despair within her, and it came out as anger.

"Wait just a minute!" she cried, and he turned back irritably. "You told me Flagstaff—this isn't

Flagstaff!'' she accused angrily. "How am I supposed to get into town?"

He scowled at her, obviously impatient to be away from her and the truck and all that reminded him of the tedious and frantic past twenty-four hours. "Hell, lady, I'm not a taxi service!" he returned, fatigue breaking his own temper and roughening his voice. "I got you here, didn't I? I told you this was my stop for the night—what do you want from me?" Then with a tight, angry breath, he turned away. "Just do as you're told, will you?" he demanded over his shoulder. "I'm too tired and grimy and hungry to argue with you now—we'll talk about it later!"

She got up on her knees and shouted out the open door after him, "Just what am I supposed to do at a truck stop ten miles from town?"

Camp whirled, anger and impatience evident in every tight line of his body, a totally exhausted man who had been pushed to the breaking point. His eyes blazed but his voice was deceptively smooth as he said coolly, "Seems to me that's the perfect place for a cute little trick like you. Why don't you see if you can get one of your Johns to drive you into town—I just don't have the time."

Fury leaped to her throat and choked her—fury and hurt and burgeoning despair, and if she could have she would have thrown something at him. For a short time today she had thought they had reached an understanding, she had almost come to like him, and worse, much worse, she had come to depend upon him—but he was no different from all the rest. He was tossing her aside like a piece of used tissue, worthless and forgotten, and she wanted to hit him. She wanted to beat her fists against him and rake her nails across his face until they drew blood and in the process expiate all her hatred and all her hurt and all her fear.

But she was not to be allowed even that small satisfaction. Perched precariously as she was on the edge of the seat, had she so much as moved she would have tumbled out the door six feet to the concrete. All she could do was scream after him, her voice tight and shaking with helplessness and rage, "Maybe I will!"

Once again he turned sharply on his heel to look back at her, and the raw impatience in his eyes seemed to be, for a moment, softened by something that might well have been regret. He drew a breath and she thought he would say something, but then his face hardened, his lips compressed, and he turned and walked away.

Somehow the sight of him walking away from her with such firm ground-eating strides was worse than all the rest. She knelt there at the open door and watched him until he rounded the corner of the low, neon-lit building and her hot blurred vision caused all the colors and the disinterested passing figures to blend and streak together, and then she turned to crawl miserably over the seat. She did not know why she did that. It was obvious she couldn't stay here. This was the end of the line for them, she was on her own, and what she should really be doing was finding

her way to the nearest mission or Salvation
Army. But, with the instinctive movements of a
wounded animal seeking privacy, she crept onto
the mattress and buried her face in the pillow that
smelled of male aftershave and sleep, and she
couldn't hold it back any longer; she started to
cry.

She cried for trust betrayed, she cried for
dreams lost. She cried for Peter who had claimed
to love her one moment and then tried to sell her
the next; she cried for a tiny attic apartment that
had been her home for the past three years—the
only home she had ever really known—for the
gaily patterned beanbag furniture she had sewn
herself, and for the yellow calico placemats shaped
like butterflies that had decorated her dining
room table. She had rescued that table from the
curb when someone had thrown it out, had ham-
mered and nailed and stained it antique red and
scavenged all over town for chairs to match. She
had loved that table. She loved the loft bed that
she had built herself and all her plants...dozens
of them, ranging from tiny flowering cacti and Af-
rican violets to a lustily sprawling Boston fern she
had named Charlie. All those things she had so
lovingly collected and cherished over the years,
the things that gave her a sense of identity and
worth and belonging...all gone because she had
wanted so desperately to believe that someone
loved her.

She cried, suddenly and unexpectedly, for the
remembered terror of the near rape. Like the

tears themselves, she had so successfully re-pressed the emotions surrounding that incident that she had not, until this moment, realized how frightened she had really been. She felt the rough hands and saw the gleaming eyes and a cold shud-der shook her like the reflex to retch. If Camp hadn't come along . . . if Camp hadn't come along she might, at this moment, be lying dead or dying alongside that Nevada highway, but would she really be any worse off than she was now?

Dusty cried because she was tired, so tired of fighting and scraping and clawing to survive, and she didn't think she could face starting over. And the vision of Camp's strong back moving away from her kept haunting the front of her mind, spurring fresh hot agonizing tears, she couldn't make that picture go away. He had been kind to her, he didn't have to be, but he had. And now it was over, finished, he was rid of her and glad of it, and what had she expected? She had been noth-ing but trouble for him and he had been more patient with her than she deserved, but it was such a lonely, cold feeling to be cast upon the side of the road like the piece of trash he thought she was.

She cried until her stomach hurt and her voice was hoarse, but still the dry wracking sobs would not leave her. They were torn from the center of her without conscious control and every one was a new exercise in agony of body and soul. She cried tears for all the times she had been too proud and too brave and too stubborn to cry before; her face was swollen and aching and exhaustion pounded at her, but still she could not stop.

It must have been a long time that she lay there, victim of nature's own painful therapy, she had no way of knowing. She only knew that eventually, at some point in time, Camp was kneeling beside her. He said nothing, he did not try to comfort or to call attention to himself, it was as though he recognized the inevitability of this basic need and would do nothing to try to stem it. After a time he simply lifted his hand to her hair, and the soothing stroking motions of his large hand over her head were both awkward and gentle; strangely therapeutic. And eventually, at last, the agony inside her died down and drained away into sporadic dry hiccoughs and an occasional reflex shudder. She felt numb and purged, an empty vessel waiting to be filled, too weary even to care whether that filling would be happiness and promise, or only more pain.

With an effort, she turned her head on the pillow and opened her bruised eyes a crack. A jean-clad hip and thigh filled her vision and she could not make her eyes travel further. She felt Camp's hand drop lightly onto her shoulder. "Listen, kid," he said quietly, "you can ride with me to Santa Fe if you want. At least it will give you something to do while you make some plans."

She turned over on her back and looked at him with swollen, apathetic eyes, not caring in the least that her face must look like it belonged to the victim of some horrible traffic accident and her supine, wretched position was both undignified and vulnerable. She noticed vaguely that he had showered and changed, his hair was light and shiny and the beard was gone, the western-stitched calico and denim shirt was fresh and attractive. She thought she must have been lying there crying for almost an hour.

"Come on," he said, pulling her to a sitting position. Nothing in his voice or manner indicated that he had just witnessed anything unusual, he was calm and matter-of-fact. "Go take a shower. I got you some things you might need." He pushed a paper bag into her hand. "A toothbrush and comb and things, and here"—he turned and took a pair of jeans and a T-shirt from a box—"you can wear these."

She accepted the clothes and the bag of toiletries numbly, and, after a second or two, felt a faint stirring of life begin again. She looked at the white T-shirt he had given her and then at him, and she said, "I'd rather have a regular shirt."

His grin was quickly amused, managing to be at the same time both rakish and reassuring. She almost felt the urge to respond. He said, "That's a waste of nature's gifts." But he pulled a red-checkered cotton shirt off a hanger and handed it to her. "I'll meet you inside. Don't take too long. And," he reminded her as he climbed back over the seat, "don't forget to put those sneakers on."

As she walked painfully across the asphalt toward the ladies' showers, she began to feel as though she might just make it. Strangely, that feeling had a lot to do with the little bag of essentials he had bought for her.... He had made those purchases when her last words to him had given him every reason to believe she would not be there when he got back, and when his to her had indicated he would be happy if she were not. Yet he had been thinking of her. For some totally inexplicable reason, that seemed to make all the difference in the world to her, at that moment.

The improvement a shower made in her disposition and outlook on life was unbelievable. That, and the fact that he had said she could come with him to Santa Fe. Had he really meant it, or was it something he had just said to comfort her and was by now regretting? Santa Fe or Flagstaff, it really didn't make any difference, she knew, but somehow the simple fact that he had offered gave her courage to face whatever lay ahead. And it felt good to be clean. She brushed her teeth and towel dried her hair to only slightly damp natural waves, and decided she really didn't look too much the worse for wear. Her face was pale with strain and fatigue and her eyes were still swollen and an unsightly red, but at least she looked as though she was ready to join the world of the living again. His jeans had to be cuffed up six inches, they were tight on her thighs and simply wouldn't button at all over her hips, but at least they were clean, and when she wore the shirt untucked over them she was covered decently. His sneakers fit her like snowshoes but her feet, especially without the bandages, were too raw and lacerated to manage the pavement without them. She wadded up the tattered green dress and left it in the trash can, and that was the first of her losses about which she felt no regret.

The truck stop was large and modern, with a gift shop leading the way to a spacious, well lit and presently crowded restaurant. The occupants of the restaurant were mostly male and of every variety, from big and burly to lean and mean, from boisterous cowboys to tired looking road jockeys. Instinctively she hated the place. Dusty knew what she looked like in Camp's tight jeans and thigh-length shirt, she knew the kind of glances she was drawing as she walked with as much grace as possible across the room. Several men grinned at her and one even spoke to her. Her cheeks were flaming and nervousness churned in her stomach as she searched the room somewhat frantically for Camp. When she finally saw him at a table at the back of the room, he was talking and laughing with a waitress, and he did not notice her. She made her way quickly to his table and tried not to look as conspicuous as she felt.

She slid into the chair opposite him but not before his eyes had a chance to scan the figure-hugging jeans and the unmistakable curves of her bust and waist, which the loose shirt did not hide nearly as well as she had hoped. In his eyes was the same gleam of appreciation she had seen from all those other men in the room, the same single-minded recognition she had seen hundreds of times before ... but strangely, from him, it did not seem quite so offensive. It only made her mildly uneasy, almost flustered.

She said, "The jeans are too tight." And she could have bitten her tongue for saying it. She felt her cheeks redden.

He looked at her knowingly, a small smile playing at the corner of his lips. "Yes," he agreed, "I guess they would be."

She tried valiantly to regain control of herself, to summon up one of those scathing put-downs that ususally came so easily to her at such occasions, but in the end all she managed was a rather irritable, "Will you please stop looking at me like that?"

Camp's eyes wandered back to her face, but far from being relieved, that only made her heart beat faster. "Like what?"

"Like—like...." Dusty floundered helplessly. Yes, like what? He was looking at her like a man looks at a woman, there was pleasure and approval in his eyes, but it was not the same look those other truckers had given her. It was not a leer, there was none of the nastiness or sneakiness in his eyes she had learned to associate with other men. He looked at her and he made no attempt to disguise the fact that he was thinking bedroom thoughts, but she was not as offended as she should have been. She was only nervous, and slightly embarrassed, and if she were completely honest with herself, a little excited. She finished at last, inadequately and in hardly more than a mumble, "Like—you're a man and I'm a woman."

His eyes were amused. "I guess I was a little slow in picking up on that," he admitted. "You'll have to excuse me for not noticing sooner, but I've had a lot on my mind. So now that I've noticed"—he refused to let the subject drop—"why does it embarrass you?"

She jerked her eyes up to him defiantly. "I am not embarrassed!" But her flaming cheeks denied the words.

He seemed to find her blush fascinating, and was determined to prolong it. "You're a beautiful woman," he told her, and his eyes went over her with frank assessment, unhurriedly and appreciatively. Her skin tingled everywhere his eyes touched, and the flush that burned her face seemed to spread downward over her chest, prickling at her breasts, warming her stomach. "Your figure was made for tight jeans and cut-off T-shirts, and why you're trying to hide it in that big shirt of mine I can't guess." His gaze returned to her face. "Why should it bother you that men look at you? You should be used to it by now."

Dusty laced her hands together deliberately in her lap and knew that playing coy with him would only give him a sense of false advantage she could not afford. She did not want him to think she was being provocative or feigning blushes to add allure, certainly the last thing she intended to do was issue him an open invitation like that. The sooner this matter was dealt with, the better, and she would rest a lot easier when they both knew where they stood. "That's just it," she told him coolly, meeting his gaze with a calmness that no way matched the redness of her cheeks. "I am used to it, and it gets to be a bore, if you want to know the truth. Men look at me and they could care less whether I even have a head, much less a brain. Would *you* like to go through life knowing that people think the only thing you're good for is something even the lowest form of animals can do without even thinking?" Her voice was beginning to become heated with emotion, her hands tightened in her lap. "For goodness' sake, even an amoeba can have sex!"

The sensual gleam in his eyes quickly changed to a spark of amusement, and he corrected, "Not precisely. Amoeba reproduce asexually by mitosis. But I see your point. I guess most people don't realize the disadvantages of being a beautiful woman."

She frowned uncertainly, grateful for the slow draining of heat from her face now that the conversation was on a more impersonal level. "I'm not beautiful," she said, and she glanced at him to reassure herself that he was still looking at her, still interested in what she had to say. He was, and the pleasure that filled her with that fact was strange and welcome. "I don't know why—men look at me like they do. I suppose..." She could not believe that she was actually putting this into words for a man, and more, that he was actually listening. She shrugged self-consciously. "I suppose there must be something about me that makes people—men—think I'm a tramp. It's always been that way. Even you," she accused, sharp-eyed. "When we first met you couldn't imagine that I was anything other than a hooker."

Camp opened his mouth for a defense, but then dropped his eyes briefly in concession. He couldn't deny it, and she did not expect him to.

Again she shrugged, toying with her water glass. "I don't know what it is. I've tried to figure it out. It's nothing I do, so it must be the way I look. Not beautiful"—she met his gaze frankly—"just sexy."

There was a small smile on his lips, but his expression was thoughtful. Dusty could not identify the warm full feeling within her that was a response to him, to his listening to her with intelligence and sensitivity, to his genuine consideration of her opinion. She had never talked to any man like this before. No one had ever listened to her before as though she had anything intelligent to say. She could not have imagined what a wonderful feeling it was to be treated like a real person by a man—and, moreover, by a man who had already admitted he found her attractive. It was such an incredibly good sensation she found herself wondering how she had lived this long without it.

He said after a moment, seriously, "I see what you mean. Sexy is nice, but beautiful is something else. It's something you don't always see with your eyes. But you shouldn't be ashamed of your body, Dusty."

Again she felt her cheeks pinken. She had

thought she had safely steered the subject onto neutral ground, but it was far more disturbing to have him talk in such a frank, serious manner about her body than to endure his insinuating looks. She looked away uncomfortably.

His soft laugh snapped her eyes back to him again, and he was leaning back against the booth, one hand resting around his beer mug, the relaxed amusement in his face seemed to be directed more at himself than at her. "I never would have thought I'd be having a conversation like this with one of the sexiest"—he placed slight emphasis on that word—"women I've seen in a long time. It's not exactly what I had in mind."

She didn't bother to ask what he had had in mind; his eyes told her. She tried not to be too disappointed. He was only a man, after all, just like every other man. She shrugged and looked away. "It's a first for me too" was all she said, and there was a brief silence in which she avoided looking at him, almost afraid of what she would find there. For the first time she allowed herself to consciously worry about what he had in mind for her. True, for the past day he had made no suggestive moves, even though she had been ready and waiting for them. But, as he had already admitted, he had had other things on his mind. Now, if they continued their journey together... was *that* why he had invited her to stay with him? She hated the ugly suspicion but she could not deny it. What other reason would any trucker want a woman on the road with him?

His next words were surprisingly casual, "Anyway," he said, sipping his beer, "you look a lot better now with all that goo washed off your face. You smell better too."

She glared at him. "Thanks," she said shortly, "so do you."

He grinned. "I was referring to that perfume you were wearing," he pointed out mildly. "It must have had the half-life of skunk oil and smelled a lot like kerosene. Reminded me of a cat house I was in once in New Orleans," he mused. "The whole place went up in flames one night when someone left a lighted cigarette next to a bottle of body oil. The mayor was most upset."

He was trying to make her smile and she determinedly fought it. "The mayor?" she returned archly, with a great display of indifference.

"He was inside at the time," Camp informed her blandly, and she had to bring her hand up quickly to hide the tightening smile at the corner of her lips.

"Aha, caught you," he said triumphantly. His eyes twinkled. "Two smiles in eighteen hours. That's not bad."

His attention was distracted then as the waitress returned with the steak platters. His attention, thought Dusty, was easily distracted. And what was it she felt with the grin he gave the buxom redhead, the words he murmured as she leaned deliberately over him, which Dusty could not hear, and the way the girl giggled and slapped his hand...? Jealousy? Or simple disgust at the

meaningful glance that passed from the eyes of
the waitress to Camp as she turned with a deliberate twitch of her hip? It was a definite "I'll see
you later" look, and Dusty could not miss the way
that Camp's eyes followed the swing of the
woman's retreating figure all the way across the
room. Yes, she decided somewhat bitterly. It was
disgust.

When they were alone again Dusty looked
down at the steaming steak and discovered she
did not have much of an appetite. There was a
small knot of nervousness in the pit of her stomach that was beginning to feel like dread. A moment ago she had felt as though all her problems
were solved, or at least postponed, but now she
must once again face a few unpleasant realities...
not the least of which was the matter of Camp's
payment for the ride. She had never before had to
say no to a man before he asked—or made de-
mands—she did not know how to approach it
now. And if she did say no she had very little
doubt she would find herself stranded at this
truck stop ten miles outside of Flagstaff once
again at the mercies of her own wit and courage,
and she did not know which would be worse.

But then her small chin lifted defiantly, she
looked at Camp without seeing him, and when he
happened to glance up he was puzzled by the hard-
ness that had come into her eyes.

"What's wrong?" he put down his knife and
fork. "Don't you like steak? Or..." His smile
was small and mocking. "Are you one of those

liberated women who takes it as an insult when a man orders for her?''

One thing she knew for certain. She had never resorted to selling herself to any man and she would not begin now. She supposed she had been in worse fixes than this...only it seemed, as she sat at the table in the bright, noisy restaurant with threatening uncertainties all around her and the only bit of stability in her entire world encased in the form of the man across from her, that she just couldn't remember any of them.

She started to speak, but something about the utter lack of guile in his amused face melted the cold resolve that had started to flow through her veins. Why had she never noticed before what a nice looking man he was? *Nice* looking. That was a term she could not remember ever having applied to a man before. The face that had been obscured by scraggly stubble was pleasant and open, with well-defined bone structure and easily curving lips...nice lips. Camp's hair was soft and fluffy and seemed to catch the light as it curved around his face and fell casually over his forehead. The collar of his shirt was open to the beginning of a tuft of sandy brown hair in the hollow of his collar bone, and it glistened against his bronze throat. She suddenly understood why that waitress had looked at him so and the understanding generated a brief and inexplicable spark of hurt in her chest. He was not only attractive, he was *nice*, and how could she sit here and coldly accuse those friendly blue eyes of plotting prostitution?

In the end she dropped her gaze, toying with her fork, and it was a moment before she said, with much less conviction than she had planned—"Look . . . I've been thinking. It was nice of you to offer to take me with you to Santa Fe, but—you really don't have to. I mean, there's nothing there that isn't here and"—she trailed off, growing increasingly uncomfortable beneath the gaze she could feel but would not face.

The silence at last forced her to look up, and it was just in time to catch Camp's eyes as they swept around the room filled with men and then narrowed on her. The conclusion he had reached was unmistakable, and there was ice in the blue depths of his eyes. He said, very smoothly, "Made other plans, have you?"

"No!" Dusty's response was quick and instinctive, and so was the hurt that flashed in her face. Both were too genuine to be less than convincing, and the ugly coldness slowly left his eyes. "It's just"—she picked at her paper napkin disconsolately, weary of defending herself and pretending with him—"I don't know what I'm going to do. . . ." she said simply, tiredly. "But it's not your problem. A few hundred miles won't make any difference."

He sat back, looking at her with eyes that were clear and steady and in some strange way gentle. "Look," he said, "I don't mind the company. As long as you stay out of trouble and don't try to claw my eyes out while I'm behind the wheel we should get on okay. It's up to you, but the offer's still open.''

But just what *was* the offer? She hated it but she had to know. She met his eyes coolly and inquired, "And just what do you expect in return?"

For a moment he simply looked at her, his face unreadable, and then he smiled. "You know something, Dusty?" he replied companionably. "I think a lot of your problem has to do with what you think of yourself. You try believing you're worth something and you might be surprised at the respect you get.''

He turned his attention back to his meal, but she would not be distracted that easily. Her nervous hand had crumpled the paper napkin into a ball and now tightened about it unconsciously. She insisted steadily, "You didn't answer my question."

He returned her gaze with eyes that were clear and unwavering and told her absolutely nothing. "Let's cross that bridge when we come to it, shall we?" he suggested easily. And then, without giving her a chance to respond or retaliate, he said briskly, "Don't spend all night over your dinner. We're out of here at five o'clock in the morning and it'll be a long time before you see a meal like this again, so enjoy it while you can."

She hesitated for just another moment, then she determinedly picked up her fork. All right, she had tried. He couldn't say he hadn't been warned if he tried to collect on expectations she had no intention of fulfilling. Besides, he was right about one thing. She had better enjoy it all while she could: the free meal, the ride, his protection and good humor. The time for all of them was limited.

When they left the restaurant Camp put his arm around her shoulders in a very proprietorial way, and Dusty could not resent the gesture. He knew that the attentions of the other men bothered her, and by marking her as his own he was protecting her. She was grateful not only for the thought, but for the way he made his intent clear by dropping his arm once they were out of the restaurant. She was surprised when he placed his hand instead on her back and guided her into the gift shop.

There he made a few quick purchases which included, to her great delight, a pair of soft beaded moccasins for her. The package label said they were hand sewn at a Seminole reservation, but she did not care whether it was true or not. They were beautiful, and he had bought them for her, and she loved them.

At the counter he asked her if there was anything else she needed. There were a lot of things she would have liked—fingernail polish remover for her chipped nails, lipstick, even a paperback book or two, but the only thing she felt right about requesting was a package of gum. Perhaps that would help allay the queasiness that always assailed her while traveling.

"I've got a few more things to stock up on," he told her, handing the package and the keys to her. "You go on back to the truck."

Oh yes, the waitress. Dusty should have been

cheered by the fact that, for this night at least, he had found someone else to entertain him, but she was not. She found the picture of him in bed with that overly made-up redhead mildly disgusting, very unsettling. She turned away quickly and her voice was a little stiff as she said, "Right." But then she could not resist tossing dryly over her shoulder, "I hope your shots are up to date."

Quick surprised laughter sprang to his eyes. "What?"

She faced him down coolly. "You never can tell what kind of"—she hesitated pointedly over the word—"diseases you might pick up in a place like this."

He only laughed harder. "Get back to the truck," he said.

She was depressed as she climbed inside and found the interior light switch. She unpacked the purchases and even her pleasure in the gift of moccasins had diminished. What had she gotten herself into? She must have been crazy to think she could travel all the way to Santa Fe with him and not be asking for more trouble than she was already in. She was only postponing the inevitable, anyway. What had made her think she would be safer with a maverick truck driver she did not even know than out there on the streets on her own? What made her think she would even be more comfortable?

She was sitting on the mattress, reapplying the first-aid ointment to her feet, when she heard the door open. She twisted around in surprise, and said the first thing that came into her mind. "What are you doing back so soon?"

He passed more packages over the seat to her, and then climbed over himself. "I'm going to bed. What did you think?"

Something tightened in her stomach and it was hard to swallow. "I—I thought..."

"I know what you thought," he replied, kneeling to put the packages of food away in the cooler, "and you've got a dirty mind. Why that surprises me, I don't know."

Dusty bit back a retort in favor of more pressing concerns. "You're—sleeping here?"

She watched him with eyes that were wide and wary as he stood and zipped up the vinyl curtain that separated the front from the back of the rig, closing off the windows and insuring privacy. The lift of his eyebrow was mildly challenging as Camp turned and began to unbutton his shirt. "You have a better idea?"

Her eyes were fixed magnetically on the lean brown hands that worked the buttons of his shirt, on the golden expanse of flesh that was rapidly being exposed. Her heart began to thud noticeably in her chest, her palms felt damp. Why was she so unprepared for this? How had he caught her off guard? And why was she finding it so incredibly difficult to summon up harsh scathing words of refusal and simply get up and climb out of the truck? But the only thing she could manage was a rather childish, very confused, cry of, "But where will I sleep?"

"I love it," he groaned in low amusement. "A woman walks in and immediately assumes the right to push a man out of his own bed." He stripped off his shirt and tossed it over the rack, where it hung by a sleeve. Camp had a magnificent chest, smooth golden skin with well defined breast muscles covered by the soft mat of light brown hair. The sight of his partial nudity made Dusty's heart beat faster—with nervousness and fear, she was sure—and her breathing escalated slightly. When he sat down beside her to pull off his boots she inched away automatically, but her eyes were captured by the way the taut muscles of his upper arms bunched and moved inside the blue-veined sheath of skin as he tugged and pulled and finally released one boot, then the other, and tossed them out of the way. He said, "I really don't care where you sleep. I wouldn't suggest the front seat; you'll wake up thinking you've died and wishing you had. And," he added matter-of-factly, eyes perfectly implacable, "if you leave this truck for more desirable sleeping quarters, you can forget about coming back."

He stretched out on the bed beside her and she quickly moved away to make room for his long legs. The scent of his mild aftershave was on his skin and the small living space was suddenly very warm. Was that his ultimatum, then? She must either make a decision now or forever hold her peace. . . . Camp folded his hands behind his head, and his eyes were totally expressionless.

There was something intriguingly sensuous

about the way his muscles stretched over a taut rib-cage to a flat abdomen, the curling pattern of body hair beneath his arms and the light triangular mat that covered his chest and crept into his jeans... she wondered rather incoherently whether he always slept in his jeans and then he caught her looking at him and she could not prevent the renewed pinkening of her cheeks.

A small smile tightened the corners of his lips. "Babe, you're looking at a man who's been driving forty-eight hours without a break, and I'm not going to touch you if that's what you're worried about," he said mildly. "I have no intention of starting something I can't finish. So..." he stretched to turn off the light, plunging the small space into utter and complete darkness. "Let's get some sleep. The bed's big enough for two, as long as you're not a kicker, or a thrasher."

Still Dusty sat there hesitantly in the dark, hardly daring to trust him, not knowing what to do. What choice did she have? She could take her chances with him or she could take her chances on her own; it was up to her and she did not know which she preferred. "Look," she said tightly, when at last the silence and the darkness and the indecision had stretched her nerves almost to the breaking point, "you offered to take me along, I didn't ask to come. I didn't ask anything from you, and I'm not going to pay..."

"For God's sake, lady," he interrupted harshly. His voice was sharp and impatient. "You don't owe me anything, okay? Stop treating yourself like a whore and maybe other people will too, did you ever think of that?" And then, with a short breath, he added somewhat more calmly, "Either lie down here and go to sleep or sit up all night, but whatever you do, be quiet about it will you? I'm beat."

Well, that was clear enough. She sat there for a time longer, finally deciding it would be ultimately foolish for her to sit up all night like a scout expecting an Indian attack. He was still for so long that she thought he must already be asleep, and gingerly, being very careful not to touch him, she lay down beside him on the mattress.

But Dusty couldn't close her eyes. She tried to breathe normally and to still the slow, uncomfortable pounding of her heart, but with very little success. She could feel his body heat warming the sheets beneath them and brushing over her arms, and his breathing was soft and regular near her ear. The clean masculine scent of him filled the entire cabin. She was afraid to move lest she disturb him, and yet perversely the memory of those strong bare arms kept flitting across her mind's eye, the lean muscular chest with its soft tangle of hair ... *This is not going to work*, she thought, somewhat desperately. *It simply isn't going to work. ...*

The sound of his voice made her jump. "Will you please relax?" Camp murmured drowsily. "I'm not going to sneak attack. And while I'll admit the urge to pin you down and make violent love to you is almost irresistible"—he yawned— "I'm fighting it."

She smiled in the dark, the smile spreading through her muscles and easing away the tension. After a moment she relaxed her tightly coiled position beside him and turned more comfortably on her back, closing her eyes.

"Good night," he murmured.

Again she smiled. "Good night."

"And Dusty..." The words came after such a long time that she had thought he was already asleep. She opened her eyes, even though she could not see him. "You're a sexy lady," he said, his voice low and sleep-softened, magnetically entrancing to her. "But also very beautiful."

She closed her eyes again, and fell asleep wondering why such an unexpectedly sweet sentiment should bring a prickling of tears.

Chapter Five

Dusty awoke to the sound of moving tires and country music. Eddie Rabbit again. She groaned and turned over, trying to blot out the sound with the pillow, but it was no use. She was awake now.

It was still dark when she opened her eyes, and for a moment she was disoriented. Then she realized that the divider between the front seat and the cabin was still closed—obviously he had rezipped it when he got up so that the light wouldn't wake her. Why did that small gesture of thoughtfulness make her feel so warm and content inside? Especially, she reprimanded herself with a scowl as she got up on her knees and attempted to straighten her hair with her fingers, since he had certainly spoiled the effect with that awful music.

She felt crumpled and cramped, her head was already beginning to ache with the movement of the truck, her mouth felt filthy and she was starving. She unzipped the divider and peered over the seat, squinting her eyes against the unexpected glare of the desert sun well up in the sky. "What's for breakfast?" she demanded ungraciously.

"That's what I love," he responded cheerfully. "A woman who wakes up with a smile and a bright 'Good morning' on her lips."

"Good morning," she said flatly. "What's for breakfast?"

"Breakfast was five hours ago, sweetheart," he returned with that same infuriating good humor. "I hope your dreams were worth missing it."

She felt unexpected warmth tinge her already sleep-flushed face. What *had* she been dreaming? Something about him. Something very intimate about him...something that had to do with strong brown arms and a bare chest. She turned away quickly and began to rummage in the back for her comb.

She felt better when she had straightened her hair, refolded the cuffs of her jeans, and tied the tails of the shirt into a knot low on her waist. She found a package of oranges in the food supplies he had bought last night, and when he extended his hand palm upward over the seat she tossed him one, then got another for herself.

"Feel better?" he inquired when she clambered over the seat to dispose of the orange peelings.

She shrugged noncommittally, and he glanced at her. "Four hundred miles to Santa Fe, sweetheart, and I think you'd better improve your disposition if we're going to make it."

"My disposition would be a lot better," she snapped at him, "if I didn't have to wake up to that garbage blasting from the stereo all the time." And then it struck her. Four hundred miles, that was not much at all. That was less than a day's travel. She had been so grateful for the postponement of the inevitable but in fact it had not been postponed much at all. She tried not to let the trepidation she felt show in her eyes as she glanced at him, and she ventured, much more casually than she felt, "I guess that means we'll get there today."

"Not necessarily. I'm dodging weigh stations and these back roads really eat up the time."

"Do we at least get to stop for lunch?" she inquired somewhat dryly.

"That depends," he replied. And then suddenly he glanced at her. "Let's see what kind of accountant you really are. Grab my log book and see what you can do with it."

For lack of anything better to do, she located the log book on the console between them. "What do you want me to do, doctor the figures for you?"

"If you have to." And even though the look she gave him was completely nonjudgmental, he for some reason felt compelled to defend himself. "Look honey, it's the only way we can make a living. Anyway..." He stretched one long arm behind him to rub the back of his neck. "This run has been so screwed up I doubt if there's anything I can do to save it now. Just give me some totals."

He was wearing a blue T-shirt this morning with a Coor's Beer slogan on the front, and the form-fitting garment outlined his chest muscles and left the tight, powerful arms bare. His face was shaded by a rather battered gray Stetson, and his soft blond hair curved gently over his neck. He looked fresh and well-rested from the few hours' sleep, relaxed and attractive and very male. Quickly she turned her eyes away and opened the log book.

The registry page made her smile. "Leon Campbell? *Leon*?" She shot an amused, teasing look at him. "No wonder you use a nickname."

He shrugged, not looking at her. "Blame my father. He thought it sounded noble."

There was something strange about the way he said that, and Dusty honed in on it immediately. It was a slight tightening of his face when he mentioned his father, an almost undetectable bitterness underscoring the word. There was resentment there and she did not think it had very much to do at all with the fact that his father had given him a name he did not like. And just as she was about to question, he prompted, "The figures?"

Dusty understood what he wanted the first time he explained it to her, and it seemed to surprise him that she brushed aside the helpful hints he tried to give her and asked no questions. She was in her element now, lost in the world of mathematics and equations, her mind working quickly and efficiently as she added and subtracted and divided rows of figures without error in her head, earning repeated looks of admiration from him to which she paid scant attention. It was like a multifaceted and highly complicated game requiring great skill and mathematical precision, and it fascinated her. The object, of course, was to somehow make the figures in his log book comply with the requirements of the Federal Highway Commission regarding the amount of miles allowable within the specified ten-hour driving day—which, unfortunately, they in no way did. With great skill and astuteness, Dusty managed to circumvent some of the most obvious flaws, but it wasn't enough.

"Okay," he sighed at last, "it looks like we stop for lunch. It's either take the chance on getting caught or missing my load in Santa Fe. I can always get another load, but I've got too many violations this year to tussle with the government again. How many hours do we have to kill to come in under the margin?"

She did some more rapid calculations, and told him, "Five."

He looked for a moment as though he wanted to swear. "That means we won't hit Santa Fe until after dark, which does me no good at all as far as my next load is concerned. We may as well stop for the night, too, and make the drop in the morning." Then he shrugged philosophically. "That's life, I guess. I've done worse."

Her frown was puzzled as she looked at him. "How long have you been doing this?"

"On my own? About two years. I drove for other companies before that. It was a lot easier, let me tell you."

"You don't manage your business very efficiently," she pointed out. "You could have avoided all this trouble if you had just planned your route a little in advance."

"If I'd taken the time to plan I never would have made the deadline," he retorted, and then, as he glanced at her, a rather sheepish grin drew at the corner of his lips. "Okay, so I'm not much of a businessman. But you've got to understand, I'm not really cut out for this type of work."

"Oh, yeah?" A comfortable spark of amusement flashed in her eyes as she tucked one leg beneath her and turned to look at him. "What kind of work are you cut out for?"

"None," he replied immediately. "At least"— he specified—"nothing physical. I was bred from a long line of cerebromaniacal intellectuals who made their living at other people's expense."

There was a lot to pick up on there, and Dusty's quick interest was alerted immediately. The note of bitterness in his voice was unmistakable this time, as was the slight tightening of his jaw. Somehow it did not surprise her that this man should come from a background at odds with his present occupation—hadn't she sensed, from the very first, that there was something different about him? Something about the way he spoke, or the look in his eyes . . . he was not an average trucker, although he was doing a passable job at masquerading as one. She was curious about him now, and anxious to unravel the man who dwelt inside the macho facade. She suspected that he would prove to be a puzzle as challenging as his log book had been.

"Where are you from?" she asked, remembering all too well the silence she had received for an answer the last time she had put that question to him.

But today he was in a better mood, more relaxed and at ease. He replied in a wildly exaggerated Harvard drawl, "Boston, my dear child, birthplace of patriotism, culture, civility... and the art of snobbery."

She giggled. "It doesn't sound as though you were too sorry to leave."

He turned his head just fractionally, ostensibly to view a passing billboard, and the hat shadowed his face so that she could not see his expression. He did not answer.

"Does your family still live there?" she tried again, becoming more and more anxious to draw him out.

"I don't know." His voice was curt. "I haven't seen them in five years."

She stifled a shocked breath. That anyone would willingly and cold-heartedly cut ties with a family—a real family—was beyond her comprehension. She could not restrain herself from demanding incredulously, "But—*why*? Are they—are they divorced, or... dead, or something?"

He laughed, shortly and mirthlessly. "Mama, Papa, sisters Gabrielle, Melissa, and Abigail..." His voice softened a little. "Abby is old enough to be married by now. That is"—and again his voice tightened with resentment—"if the old man let her out of the house long enough for the ceremony."

That was the second—no the third time—he had implied something unfavorable about his father. Her curiosity would not go unanswered this time. "Don't you like your father?" she inquired, concerned. "I mean, was he cruel to your sisters or—did he drink too much or beat you or something—is that why you left home?"

Once again he laughed, and once again it was an unpleasant sound. "My father—drunk—cruel—violent? Bite your tongue! My father was one of the most well-respected attorneys in Boston, a product of four generations of respected attorneys, he would never in his wildest moments even consider doing anything that approached violating the letter of the law. My father," he went on in a more even tone that was only slightly tinged with unpleasantness, "was gentle, refined, soft-spoken and civilized to a fault. He never did anything that might even remotely be considered improper and he never allowed us to, either. He was a pillar of the community, loved by widows and orphans all over the world . . . a prince among men. Yes indeed," he finished, almost to himself. The sarcasm was unmistakable. "A real prince."

The way he said that implied that he meant just the opposite, and that only confused Dusty more. This was all very difficult for Dusty to absorb—the concept of a family, loyal and undivided, a gentle life, centuries of background and permanency to support them, sisters whose names conjured up visions of hand-smocked pinafores and china tea sets... and why did he seem to hate it all so? Why had he left it all so carelessly behind when she would have given all of her dreams for just one day of belonging to a family like his? And what—what in the world was he doing driving a heavily mortgaged truck along desert highways for a living, drinking cheap beer and eating bologna sandwiches and flirting with tight-skirted waitresses in neon-lit restaurants when he could have had luxury and comfort at his fingertips? Frowning slightly with spiraling curiosity, she said, "But I don't understand. Why—"

He interrupted curtly, "Let's just drop it, okay?" And he reached for the CB mike with a tight movement of restrained anger. He spoke into it in a harsh, expressionless tone, "Breaker, breaker this is Red Horse, anybody got their ears on out there? How about a smokey report? Come on."

Though acutely disappointed by the change of subject and a little hurt by his anger, Dusty felt a giggle rise at his easy lapse into CB lingo. Although he had been monitoring the radio since she had gotten into the truck, this was the first time he had used it, and the slang that sounded so natural from the mouths of other truckers seemed outrageous when he spoke it. Dusty said, trying not to laugh out loud, "Red Horse?"

He shrugged, "I got it off a tobacco package."

And then a voice, crisp but unmistakably feminine, crackled back over the radio, "Breaker, Red Horse, this is Smokey and I've got you in my sights, come on."

For a moment he was nonplussed, and then he broke into a delighted grin. He pushed the button to a buzz of static and without preliminary jargon, exclaimed, "Hey, Cookie, is that you?"

The amused laughter that had begun died in Dusty's throat. Why should she feel that small stab of resentment toward the feminine voice that had brought that grin of pleasure to Camp's face and completely wiped away his former tension? Why should she suddenly be reminded of the way he had looked at that waitress last night?

The voice replied, "That's a big ten-four good buddy, give it a peek, come on."

Camp cast his eyes toward the large side mirror and laughed out loud. Dusty, of course, could not see the vehicle behind them that seemed to be giving him so much pleasure. He pushed the button again. "Breaker, Cookie, you're lookin' good. What brings you out this way? Come on."

"Lookin' for you good buddy as always. What're you doing on my turf? Come on."

"Seekin' the action, babe, come on."

"You found it Red Horse. Where do you lay your beautiful bod tonight? Come on."

"Double-nicklin' it all the way to Santa Fe, sweet meat. You after my tail? Come on."

"You betcha, Red Horse, give me a break, come on."

"Always willing, Cookie, catch me if you can, come on."

"Don't I wish, Red Horse, I've got a taste for something sweet but I'm over the line and out. Keep 'em moving, Red Horse, I'm out."

Camp reached overhead and gave one long blast on the mighty horn, chuckling to himself as he replaced the mike.

Dusty stirred uneasily in her seat, trying to quell the resentment she felt. Okay, so maybe he wasn't born to the trucking life, but he had never said he hadn't acquired a taste for it. Why did she keep thinking about that waitress last night? And why should she find the crude terms in which they had made their assignation so offensive? Certainly she had received more unsavory propositions in her lifetime. But, more importantly, if he intended to keep a date with "sweet meat," where did that leave her?

She tried to keep her emotions hidden as she said stiffly, "Does that mean you're going to push for Santa Fe today after all?"

He glanced at her. "What do you mean?"

"Well, I don't think Cookie-baby would be too thrilled to crawl into the back of your truck and find me there," she retorted acidly. "So unless you've changed your mind and decided to dump me on the side of the road after all, we go to Santa Fe."

He burst into incredulous, delighted, full-bodied laughter. "You think...!" But laughter choked off his words. He gripped the steering wheel as the force of it shook his arms and Dusty squirmed angrily beneath his utter and complete enjoyment of a joke she did not understand. At last he gasped, his eyes sparking still with unrestrained mirth, "For God's sake, honey, Cookie is a cop!"

She scowled at him openly. "I don't see what that has to do with anything! She certainly had a lot of interest in your 'beautiful bod' for a cop!"

Again he choked on another burst of laughter. "That was just her way of asking my destination— I've never even met the lady!"

Dusty's scowl deepened. She hated it when he laughed at her, she hated it even more when she began to suspect that she had leapt to an unmistakably wrong conclusion. "Oh, yeah?" she challenged. "You seemed to be awfully familiar with one another's 'tails' for two people who've never met!"

He couldn't seem to stop laughing. "Haven't you ever used a CB before?" His eyes were snapping with delighted amusement.

"No!" she shot back, her own eyes beginning to churn with anger and embarrassment. "And I don't see what's so damn funny!"

"You are! Trying to hide your innocence with a dirty mind—you're a fish out of water and you're too proud to admit it." And then, managing to control his amusement somewhat, he explained, "Cookie is a country policewoman on highway patrol. She dogs my tail every time I come through trying to catch me over the limit. She has a mean reputation with all the truckers so I always watch my radar on this stretch. She's never caught me and we like to needle each other when we get in range. That's all there is to it. Now..." He couldn't resist one more amused stab. "Tell me *your* version of the conversation."

Dusty looked uncomfortably out the window, trying to suffuse a dull flush. "When do we eat?" she said grumpily.

"As soon as you get rid of that damn gum," he returned implacably, but she could feel lingering amusement in his gaze. She deliberately blew a bubble and popped it.

They stopped for hamburgers outside a small town whose name Dusty did not even notice. It was of course impossible to maneuver the big rig into the parking lot, so they left it in a vacant lot and walked across the street. It was broiling hot and desert dry, but Dusty was so grateful for the opportunity to get out of the truck and actually use her legs again that she did not mind the blistering discomfort of the sun. They ate outside beneath the sparse shade of an umbrella canopy, there was not a breath of breeze and the milkshake Camp had ordered for her was warm and melted before she even tasted it.

"Do you always drive the western routes?" Dusty inquired, squinting against the glare of the sun on the concrete patio that they shared with three boisterous children whose parents dined in air-conditioned comfort inside, sending them warning scowls from the window. "Do you ever get back East?"

"Sometimes," he admitted. "I'm based out here but I go wherever I have to. Why?"

"I don't know." Her eyes moved slowly over the heat-mirrored road before them, the dry blank landscape around them, sand and sky and nothing in between. "It's just so—barren. I think I'd go crazy if I had to look at nothing but desert all day, day after day... I miss the greenery."

"Oh ho—pining away for the lush concrete jungle, are you?" he teased.

She defended, "We have trees in Central Park. Besides, I have lots of plants..." She dropped her eyes. "I mean, I had. House plants, you know. Growing things seem to make a house feel like a home."

She felt him looking at her, but she took another bite out of her hamburger, wishing she had never brought up the subject. She didn't want to start thinking again about all she had lost. She had cried all her tears last night and she would not look back again.

Then he said unexpectedly, "You'd like New England, then. Everything's green there—until September, when the whole world is on fire with more colors than you can count. Of course, come December, the landscape is about as bare as anything you see out here, but the snow almost makes up for it."

She smiled at him a little hesitantly. Once again

he was talking to her like a person whose feelings and preferences were important, and she wondered if he could possibly know how good it made her feel when he did that. "It must have been nice," she ventured, "growing up like you did ... in a real house, with a real family, in New England."

A vagueness came over his sun-lightened blue eyes, perhaps a flinch of pain, and he said absently, "I suppose it was." There was a moment in which his thoughts took him into faraway places she wanted desperately to follow. She could see him drifting away from her and the sadness and yearning which briefly swept her was the knowledge that even if she had been welcome into his secret thoughts, she would not belong....

But it was over in less than a second. Camp looked back at her and there was nothing in his eyes to indicate he had been thinking of anything more important than the way the sun shone on the sun-cracked ground across the street. He said, "Do you want to walk around awhile? We've got time to kill and I could use the exercise."

"That sounds good," she agreed enthusiastically, gathering up the paper wrappers that littered the table. Anything to postpone the return to the incessant movement of that truck and the merciless whine of country-western music.

"What about your feet?" he remembered with a sudden frown of concern as they stood.

"Oh, they're much better now," she assured

him. And she glanced at him shyly. "The moccasins help. They're soft."

He smiled at her gently, and dropped a light hand on her shoulder to guide her around an artificial cactus that bordered the patio. "They couldn't possibly be much better," he said, "but we'll walk slow and we won't go far. Not," he added with a grimace at the ruthless sun, "that we could get very far in this heat."

She agreed, and cuffed up the sleeves of her shirt above her elbows. Then she glanced back over her shoulder at the truck. "Isn't it illegal to leave it parked there?"

"Yep," he replied, and laced his fingers easily and naturally through hers as they negotiated a small dry gully. She liked the way his hand felt around hers, warm and rough. It was a companionable gesture that in some way smacked of possessiveness, and Dusty liked that too. It made her feel secure, and wanted, yet it allowed her to walk side by side with him as an equal in the way she could not have had his arm been around her waist or her shoulders. And as they walked in easy, slow silence away from the road and into the barren desert, she began to realize that there was quite a lot she liked about Camp.

He said, "What are you going to do in Santa Fe?"

A reasonable question, and one any mildly interested bystander would be prone to ask. The only trouble was, she had no answer, she had not even prepared a good lie. But there was confidence in her voice which was almost genuine as she replied, "First I'll have to find some place to stay while I look for a job. It won't take me long to find one. I've done all sorts of work..." She shot him a quick sharp glance, and qualified, "Almost all sorts." His face remained expressionless, his eyes bland and nonjudgmental. That gave her the encouragement to continue. "I probably won't stay there long. Just until I can get some stake money and a bus ticket to a bigger city where I can get a real job. I don't think I'll go back to New York. It's too expensive to live there, and I was getting a little tired of it anyway." She ventured a hesitant glance at him. "Maybe I'll try New England. Or even the South, where things stay green all year long."

His eyes were deep and probing as he slowed his steps to look at her, and alight with curiosity. "How in the hell," he inquired simply, "did you get yourself into this mess?"

He looked so genuinely interested, so concerned and willing to know, that she almost told him. It was only her natural instinct for self-preservation, that well-developed sense of wariness that automatically warned her not to share too much of herself with anyone, that kept her silent. She shrugged. "It's a long story."

"Most of them are," he murmured. They started walking again, circling back toward the truck. "You meet a lot of strange people on the road," he went on thoughtfully, "all of them with one weird tale or another to tell..." And he looked at her. His eyes were puzzled, curious, and somewhat surprised, much as they had been this morning when he had wrestled over the problem of the log book. "But you're different. You don't belong in the same class with the street people and the destitute and the hobos that are wandering the roads out here. You're too bright and talented for something like this to have happened to you."

Camp's concern touched Dusty much more than she wanted to admit. It disturbed her because she knew he said exactly what he meant and because in saying it, he had awakened something within her she had almost forgotten existed... a sense of self worth. Yet, in some strange and subtle way, he had been doing that since she had met him, seeing through the tough façade and touching the fragile shreds of her own identity, gradually drawing them back together again into a reminder of who she was and what she could do. She did not know how to answer him. How do you respond to someone who is, slowly and by particles, giving your life back to you?"

She shrugged uncomfortably, not looking at him. "I may be talented, but I'm not very bright. If I were I'd be all settled in to some cushy nine-to-five job right now instead of going back to basics the hard way."

There was a moment of silence, and there was something old in his voice as he inquired after a moment, "Is that what you want for yourself? A nine-to-five job?"

"Yeah." She smiled a little to herself. "And a house in the suburbs. You know, one of those neighborhoods where there's a swing set on every lawn and the kids ride their bikes up and down the street and play baseball in the park. A place where the morning paper always lands in the bushes and the biggest battle you fight is against crab grass. A place where you can hear the birds sing. And my own willow tree, right in the middle of the front yard. *That's* what I want, and," Dusty finished with an unconscious breath of determination, "that's what I'm going to have some day."

His eyes were unreadable, his tone strange. "I assume a husband and children are included in those plans?"

She laughed a little, embarrassed to be caught daydreaming out loud. "I guess so. I never thought too much about that part." Perhaps because she was afraid to let herself want too much. "Mostly it's just the idea of having a place to call my own, and never having to move again, you know?"

The quick shy glance she gave him was filled with an unintentional plea for understanding, and his gentle smile was her answer. "Yes," he said quietly, "I know." He looked at her for a moment as though he would say more, and something indefinable in that look made Dusty catch her breath. She couldn't move her eyes away from his for just that moment, searching them, trying to read what lay behind their lake-blue depths...was it tenderness? Or was it sadness?

What was it he saw in her face to make him look that way?

But she was not to know. They had reached the truck, and he released her hand to unlock the passenger door. Dusty would not have believed it, but she was actually glad to be back in the shelter of the truck. The sun was brutal, and she was hot and sweaty, anxious for the air-conditioned interior. The cuffs of the long-sleeved shirt had fallen down again, and the knot into which she had tied the tails had come undone sometime during the morning so that it once again fell to her thighs. The material was damp and sticky over her breasts and stomach and even her legs were drenched with perspiration.

He looked at her with sudden scrutiny. "You're going to burn up in that outfit," he said. "We're coming up on some of the hottest country in the world, you've got to think comfort first and modesty later."

She did not know what he meant by that and was not particularly anxious to find out. She turned to climb inside. "That's okay; the truck's air-conditioned."

"Nope." He caught her wrist and turned her around. "Across this stretch we run it on low if at all; we can't afford the fuel consumption." He looked her over critically. "That shirt is too hot, and you can at least cuff up the jeans."

"Yesterday you told me to keep myself covered," she blurted inexplicably, and a blue spark played in his eyes as he took the hem of her shirt and began to fold it up above her waist.

"That was yesterday," he assured her with mock sobriety, and his eyes lowered to the path of flesh he was exposing, the soft rounded abdomen that strained against the open snap of the jeans low on her hips, the surprising firm indentation of waist, the perfectly formed ribcage. He caught his breath softly. "Yesterday," he said, "I was being very selfish—and stupid." His fingers brushed against her skin as he tied the shirt into a knot high under her breasts and her own breathing became suddenly irregular. His touch, whether casual or deliberate, tingled with unexpected warmth on her moist skin, prickling nerve fibers into awareness. She knew she should step away and finish the task for herself, but she couldn't seem to manage it. She kept her eyes on his face, anxious and waiting, every part of her suddenly alive because he had touched her.

And when he lifted his eyes to hers again they were calm and steady, though there was a deep light within them that told her he, too, had found unexpected pleasure in the simple movement. Camp watched her as she watched him, carefully, curiously, as though expecting her at any moment to bolt, and he brought his fingers to the collar of the shirt and undid the button there.

One strong hand rested very lightly against the curve of Dusty's bare waist while the other very slowly released the buttons from the collar to the knotted hem below her breasts—slowly, and with deliberation, his fingers lingering with cautious boldness against each section of flesh he exposed. His eyes never left her face, they were alert and steady, searching for and absorbing her every reaction, holding her and refusing to let her break away. Her heart was pounding and she was certain he must see the pulse in her throat or feel the shaking of her ribcage with his fingers. The heat that was beginning to suffuse her in wave after slow wave was more intense and more draining than that of the sun. She tried to hide from him what his simple, perfectly innocent touch was doing to her, she kept her face expressionless and her eyes upon his and her lips closed even though it was hard to breathe. But there was nothing innocent about the way he looked at her. There was gentleness there, but behind it a purposeful intent, almost a challenge. His eyes held her steady as, the last button undone, he moved his fingers lightly up the narrow triangle of bare skin and then slowly down again, exploring by touch rather than sight, and then, very lightly, his fingers brushed and circled the fullness of her breast.

"Easy," Camp whispered at her automatic stiffening, the way one would soothe a skittish animal. His fingers hovered over her, barely touching the material, his eyes watchful and reassuring as they held hers. The hand that was on her waist moved slightly, not tightening but simply providing a light support, and he was standing very close, so that their thighs brushed and his presence engulfed her. *When had he moved so close?* Dusty wondered incoherently. Her heart was pounding erratically and the fingers that hovered above her breast held a tantalizing promise, almost drawing her fullness into their gentle cup, but she could not help it, she gasped out loud with the electric pressure of his palm atop the material. Everything within her began to pulse and shake to the choking rhythm of her heart as those fingers moved, ever so gently, in exploring warmth, there was a coiling sensation deep within the pit of her stomach as he sought and captured with utmost delicacy one surging nipple. And his eyes never left hers, with watchful gentleness absorbing her helpless and instinctual response to his tactile explorations while at the same time allowing her to see the pleasure that was growing within him. With utmost care and tenderness his thumb and forefinger tightened around her throbbing nipple and rubbed gently, the weakness and yearning that spread through her limbs was uncontrollable.

She had never experienced anything like this before. The sun was beating on her back and blurring dizziness in her head, but inside her a much more powerful flame was kindling. Dusty knew she should stop him, she *wanted* to stop him, but he had her firmly in the spell of his eyes and she could not breathe, she could not break away. It would have been so much easier had he not looked at her so, had he not been so gentle and slow, careful not to frighten her, as though he really cared how she felt, as though he would not proceed without her permission... As though he were testing something between them, no more, and would not push if she did not want it. But she did want it. It was irrational and impossible, but all Dusty could focus on at that moment was the mesmerizing, intensely escalating pleasure his fingers were creating, the touch of him and the smell of him and the warmth of his body flowing over her which made the radiating heat of the desert fade in comparison. And all she wanted was the feel of strong male thighs pressing against hers and arms drawing her into the circle of his body, holding her, touching her, pressing her into him...

Camp bent his head and Dusty felt the brush of his lips upon her collar bone. His hand moved, cupping and lifting, even as his lips moved very slowly downward and across her chest, brushing away material in their path and touching new flames upon bare skin. Her heart was slamming against her chest, her breath dried in her throat, sparks of dizziness prickled her eyes. Somehow her hand came up to his arm, an instinctual movement of support, and the sweet warmth of his bare skin surged beneath her fingers. But she made her hand tighten there, pushing at him, and she whispered hoarsely, "Camp—don't. Please. Stop..."

His lips closed over the beginning curve of her breast and hesitated there. In one moment of wildly beating pulses and twisting uncertainty she was not sure whether she wanted him to respect her request or disregard it, and the small sound she tried to bite back was indistinguishable as a protest. And then, very slowly, with straining reluctance, he moved away.

"All right." The whisper was an airy breath that chilled her skin. He straightened up, his eyes very clear and steady even above the mixture of confusion and reluctance there. Her eyes met his for just a second of confused apology and utter misery, and then she could not look at him any longer.

His hands moved to her face, cupping it gently and smoothing back her hair, and, eventually, exerting a gentle pressure that forced her to meet his eyes again. For a moment he simply looked at her, but her own emotions were in too much of a turmoil to read what might be written on his face. His smile, when it came, was meant to be reassuring, but in fact it was a little stiff. "No problem," he said softly, and he' let his hands fall. His next words were calm and matter-of-fact. "Let's get rolling."

His hands upon her waist were light and impersonal as he assisted her into the truck, but he hesitated when she was settled before closing the door. His expression was enigmatic, the patterns of sun and shadow that played over his Stetson-shielded face completely unreadable. "That was a lie, you know," he said quietly. "You are becoming a problem—one I'm not all that sure I can handle any more.'' But then he closed the door firmly, and whatever she might have said in response—if anything—died in her throat.

Chapter Six

The truck was in gear, a tape in the player and everything was back to normal. Camp took a beer from the cooler and offered her one; she refused but opened the can for him without his asking. He pulled the hat down lower over his eyes and settled back, sipping the beer. She tried to forget about what had happened in the desert. He seemed to have done so already.

It didn't take long for the incessant country music to get on her nerves, and in combination with a lingering tension born partially from pure physiology and partially from emotional confusion, her temper mounted. Every time she glanced at him, his strong corded arms seemed to leap into her vision, the sight of slim fingers resting on the steering wheel brought tingling heat to her cheeks, the body-hugging T-shirt, with its dark patches of perspiration beneath his arms and on his chest, drew her attention and wouldn't let it go. She knew if she spoke to him her words would come out harsh and stinging, and she did not think she could stand to fight with him now. But she couldn't sit there beside him in silence with Willie Nelson music setting her teeth on edge and try to pretend, as he was so successfully doing, that nothing had changed between them. She clambered over the seat with the vague idea of finding something to do to keep her busy.

Of course, she told herself with a new attempt at mature reasoning, to be perfectly realistic about the situation, nothing *had* changed between them. Camp had tried—as, being only a man, it was inevitable that he would—and he had failed. He was really being a very good sport about it. She ventured a glance at him, strong shoulders at ease behind the wheel, one brown hand now coming up to rub his neck muscles, and knew that nothing about him had changed. He still felt the same way about her he always had. She was just a woman in distress he had rescued and somehow gotten stuck with; he had admitted that first night that he had been without female companionship for some time and he was making the best of the situation. It was to be expected, and one moment of predictable intimacy between them would make no difference to him. Then why should she feel that everything was beginning to change within her?

Absently Dusty ran her finger over his collection of books. There were many more than she had originally thought, some were stacked underneath the shelf and in odd corners of the sleeping quarters, beneath boxes and lining wall space. Paperback fiction included mystery thrillers, historical sagas, westerns, science fiction and fantasy classics; the hardcover books were leather bound and looked very expensive to be treated so carelessly. Interspersed among poetry collections, literary classics, and what she assumed to be college textbooks were several volumes on law, politics, and sociology. The puzzle of Leon Campbell was becoming more and more intriguing.

She did not trust herself to pursue, with any amount of patience, the solution to that puzzle now, however, neither did she feel she could concentrate on the intricacies of a fictional plot in her present mood. She finally selected a volume of poetry and settled back on the mattress, trying to let the cadence of words override the irritation of the stereo and, much to her surprise, eventually succeeding.

She did not notice when the tape ran out, and it was the sound of Camp's voice that made her look up. "What are you reading?" he asked over his shoulder.

She got up on her knees to show the volume to him. "Yeats," she replied.

He looked surprised that she had pronounced the poet's name correctly; the common mispronunciation was "Yeets" and it was a mistake she was certain he had expected her to make. Dusty smiled a little to herself but said nothing. She supposed she would continue to surprise him in the same way he continued to surprise her because neither one of them was precisely what they appeared to be.

He invited unexpectedly, "Why don't you come up here and read out loud to me? That's one thing I never have learned how to do—read and drive at the same time. I suppose if I did I wouldn't have anything left to complain about."

She hesitated for only a moment, and then complied. For a time there was nothing but the rise and fall of her voice against the background hum of the engine and the whine of tires, and she could sense that his enjoyment of the quiet mood that spread between them was as great as her own. When she paused after a time between selections he said, "You have a pretty voice. Nice rhythm." His eyes flickered for a moment away from the road. "Nice legs, too," he added blandly.

Self-consciously she crossed her bare ankles. It had been warm in the back of the truck, and she had rolled her jeans up above her knees. Now she was both sorry and a little glad she had. She closed the book. "Where did you get all those books back there?" she inquired curiously. "Law, and history and politics . . . they're not exactly essential equipment for a trucker."

He seemed to hesitate a moment before replying, "Harvard Law School, Class of '77." His tone was brisk and the quick glance he shot her registered her shock.

"Do you mean . . ." She twisted in her seat to face him, her small brow puckered with confusion and amazement. "You're really a *lawyer*?"

The ligaments of his hands seemed slightly more prominent on the big wheel, but his voice was calm, almost nonchalant. "In a manner of speaking."

"But..." Dusty struggled to understand. "You went from practicing law to—to long-hauling... Why?"

Her intensely curious scrutiny did not miss the slight tightening of his jaw, nor the unconscious movement he made to rub his taut neck muscles. Still his voice was carefully unrevealing. "It's a long story. There were a lot of reasons."

She tried to make sense of this the best she could. "I suppose..." She ventured at last, "that sometimes there's more money in driving a truck than being a professional... especially in a profession that's oversaturated. I read somewhere that there is one lawyer for every fourteen people in America. There can't be much profit in that."

He seemed to relax. "Right," he agreed easily. "They don't tell you that when you enter law school."

"Then why did you do it?"

Instinctively she sensed she had gone one step too far. She thought he would not even bother to answer. The relief and gratitude that spread through her when he did was a warm reassurance that felt like drawing close to him. "I had some very idealistic ideas about saving the world," he said carefully, his eyes on the road. "I would have been a public defender or a legal-aid representative... of course, my father would have no part of that. You see, it's traditional to produce at least one lawyer every generation, but never had tradition allowed for that lawyer to serve the needs of the people. The Harvard Law degree was designed to be decorative, not functional. So I ended up in my father's corporation; about as useful as a Hepplewhite table. One thing led to another, and..." He trailed off, shrugging.

There were so many gaps in his story, so many things left untold, that Dusty was more confused than ever. She could understand his need to feel useful, she could even understand, just barely, his resentment at being kept under his father's thumb, but why had he just walked away instead of staying to fight when he had so much worth fighting for? She would not push him on that point, but her need to know more about his family, his home, his background was irresistible. Just hearing him talk about it conjured up visions of security and beauty and permanence for her, hearing him talk about it was probably as close as she would ever come to the real thing. The need to see with her mind's eye again the graceful, refined home, the genteel family steeped in generations of tradition and sameness was like a thirst to her, or the craving for something sweet; it was the need to hungrily gather all his memories as a store against the harsh times that lay ahead for her, and it gave her the courage to request, rather shyly, "Would you—tell me more about your family? Your house, how you grew up, Boston..."

She knew immediately it was not a request that was going to be granted. The muscle tightened in his jaw again, sealing from her his secret parts, and he said shortly, "It's a dull story."

The disappointment tasted bitter in her throat, she lowered her eyes and missed the puzzled look that crossed his face when he caught it. She absently fingered the volume of Yeats in her lap and she said after a moment, quietly, "Why do you hate your father?"

The tension that replied spoke voluble waves; she was afraid to look at him because she knew the anger she would find there. After a moment he replied shortly, "I don't hate him. My father was a very rigid man—in his interpretation of the law, in his expectations from people. I was a rebel, a maverick. I couldn't seem to do anything to please him, and he had no tolerance for me. We didn't get along. That's all." And then he put another tape in the deck, and the subject was closed.

Miles piled up in silence, and Dusty tried not to be too dispirited. She would not push him. They both had their secrets.

He talked with some trucker friends on the CB. He played endless recordings about hard times and the traveling life, after a while, apparently growing bored with his own company, he began to tell her entertaining stories of little consequence about his adventures on the road. And after a while, he even made her laugh.

They stopped for the night at a well-equipped rest stop not far outside Santa Fe. This one was heavily trafficked by passenger cars and campers which stopped for a break or an evening picnic, and there were three other big rigs which were apparently parked for a longer duration. Camp told her they would be able to shower here, and that in itself was a buoy to her mood. Dusty was hot and sticky and grimy from their walk at lunch, and a cool shower was just the thing she needed to restore her equilibrium.

As they gathered up their toilet articles from the back, Camp handed her a fresh pair of jeans and a T-shirt. "Wear it," he said in a tone that allowed no argument. "You've been stifling all day in that long-sleeved thing, and I promise to do my best to keep my animal lust under control."

She tried not to smile as she accepted the shirt meekly.

Camp walked with her to the showers, a courtesy she thought was designed to shield her from what he suspected might be the uncertainties of such an isolated spot. It was little things like that, Dusty reflected as she stripped off the worn clothes in the privacy of the shower stall—thoughtful little things that he seemed to do automatically and without thinking—that made him so special, so . . . different. And so endearing.

She allowed only a trickle of hot water to run through the cold, and the shower was stimulating, cleansing, and refreshing. She felt born again as she blotted her cool skin dry and combed the tangles out of her shiny clean hair. She stepped into jeans and her moccasins, and pulled on the T-shirt. It was white, with a black script slogan on the chest that read, "I love Beethoven." On the back was a pen-sketch of the artist, and she smiled a little when she saw it.

She waited for her hair to dry into damp curls around her face, and Camp was waiting for her when she came outside. Immediately and predictably, his eyes swept over her, but she tried to take it in stride, tried to deny the treacherous and uncontrollable little thrill that shivered through her when he looked at her like that.

"Do you really?" she said brightly, a little nervously.

Bright blue eyes skimmed across her face, a smile played with his lips. "Really what?"

"Love Beethoven."

His eyes fastened deliberately and lingeringly upon her chest again. "More and more," he assured her, and then he stepped forward and took her towel and soiled clothes from her. "I brought you something," he said, and placed a styrofoam cup in her hand.

The cup was filled with damp sand, and nestled within the sand was a baby cactus. "I thought it would satisfy your craving for green things for the time being," he explained negligently. "I looked for a philodendron, but they were fresh out."

Her throat convulsed unexpectedly and she felt the warmth of tears surprise her eyes before she determinedly blinked them back. Still, she did not trust her voice for a time, and she kept her eyes fixed on the small gift that encompassed, in its thoughtfulness, more value than a handful of diamonds.

When at last she spoke it was in a nonchalant tone that was valiantly designed to hide her weakness. "I had lots of cacti at home," she said, and they began walking toward the truck. "I don't know why I liked them so much; they've got to be the ugliest thing ever created."

"Oh, I don't know." Camp looped his arm casually over her shoulders. "I think the cockroach runs a close tie for that. Or the salamander. Now there's a freak of nature if ever there was one; slimy eyeless monsters." Dusty giggled and was grateful for the small release of emotion that gesture afforded. She was brimming over with happiness and contentment and other things too numerous and too effervescent to define. "Anyway..." His fingers brushed through her hair, separating damp tendrils from drying ones, ruffling and disordering it carelessly as though for the simple pleasure of watching it fall back into place. "Cactus have their own strange beauty—survivors in a wasteland, a testament to life amidst nature's destruction..." His hand rested against her neck, she could feel his eyes upon her. "Courageous and indestructible, a jewel in the desert... like you."

Dusty looked up at him, a sudden wonder catching in her throat, and his eyes were very solemn, very deep blue. She searched and tried to memorize everything that was in his eyes, wanting to see things and believe in things she had never imagined before... and then it was gone.

He said, his hand dropping casually to her back,

"Shall we retire to the veranda for mint juleps and canapés?"

Her laugh was a little forced. "How about pressed turkey sandwiches and corn chips under the shade of . . ." She lifted the cup to him. "This cactus?"

He shrugged agreeably. "It's better than nothing."

Cool air came abruptly with the lowering sun; they bought icy cold soft drinks from the machine and feasted on sandwiches and Twinkies at one of the stone tables near the truck. Afterward, Camp brought out his guitar and entertained a group of children—as well as their parents—with some easy country tunes that he played and sang quite well. Dusty, too, was enthralled, loving the sound of his voice and the haunting quality of guitar strings on the still night air, shivering to the ghostly sadness of "Streets of Laredo" and thrilling to the upbeat rhythm of "If I Had a Hammer." When at last, growing tired, he trailed off into random chords and absent classical progressions, she teased him, "Where did the Harvard boy learn songs like that?"

He grinned at her and set the guitar aside. "The same place I learned to drive a truck." He reached for her hand. "It should be cool enough to go inside now. Do you want to watch some television?"

"All the comforts of home, eh?" Her hand joined his naturally.

"It *is* home," he reminded her easily, and once

again Dusty was puzzled and a little shaken by the fact that anyone would choose this life of constant movement and no certainties; that anyone could with willing conviction call life on the road home.

Tonight, however, the conveniences of home were mitigated by poor reception, and after a while, weary of fighting it, Camp turned the small television set off. Dusty was sitting cross-legged on the mattress, combing her hair, and he sat beside her, grimacing a little as he rubbed the back of his neck. "Does your neck hurt?" she inquired.

"Yeah," he sighed, irritably working the muscles. "It gets stiff sometimes; I thought the shower would help, but it didn't."

She volunteered without hesitation, "Would you like me to massage it for you?"

The quick gratitude in his eyes eradicated any opportunity to renege on the offer, even if she had been so inclined. "That would be nice," he said, and he stretched out face-down on the mattress as she moved toward him.

At first she was glad only to be doing something for him in small repayment for all he had done for her. She was gratified by his murmured, "Nice," and by his monosyllabic sound of encouragement when her hands moved to his shoulders. She had never done this for anyone before, and she was glad to be able to bring him some small comfort, pleased that he appreciated her efforts. But then, inevitably, she became increasingly aware of the tantalizing strength of male muscles beneath her fingers, of the smoothness and warmth of the skin of his neck, the suppleness which yielded and surged beneath her ministrations. Nothing stirred outside, the interior of the truck was shrouded in softly lit intimacy, and the silence breathed with the power of the basic communication between one body and another.

He was pliable, silent, and relaxed beneath her hands. He made no sound or movement to intrude upon her fantasies, and fantasies they were, on a dim subconscious level... having to do with the length of his strong body stretched out before her, the brush of blond hair against her fingers, the memory of the way his bronzed face crinkled in the sun, the look in his eyes when he had given her the cactus, the way it had felt when he touched her... Absently, her hands slowed and stopped moving altogether, simply resting atop his shoulders, and she looked at him.

Camp turned over slowly. His smile was gentle and drowsy, his eyes sleep-hazy and subtly sensuous. "You have good hands," he murmured, and gathered one of them within his fingers, holding it against his chest. "Strong... but soft." One finger traced a light pattern over the delicate veins on the back of her hand, grazing across the knuckles and exploring the indentations. His other hand stretched to her face, a finger lightly touching the corner of her eye. "Pretty eyes," he said softly. "Innocent, vulnerable, wise... and what you can't hide in your eyes is so much more alluring than your sexy body or your tough-guy act..." His eyes were now a little puzzled. "Why do you do that, Dusty? Don't you know that what's inside of you is the most fascinating part of you?"

She shook her head a little, mesmerized by the touch of his hand against the side of her face and by the deep, warm look in his eyes. Her voice sounded a little hoarse. "I—don't know. Habit, I guess."

He smiled, very softly. The smile was more in his eyes than on his lips. The hand that held hers released it and slipped around her waist, the other arm encircled her shoulders. He said, "Come here." and she did not resist, her muscles melting into the gentle pressure of his as he drew her down to him.

His lips met hers softly, a delicate probing and tasting that was like a jolt of color to her deadened senses. Every nerve fiber flared into helpless awareness with the contact of his mouth upon hers, unexpectedly brilliant, powerfully moving. Her skin tingled, as though every pore had suddenly, and without reservation, opened to receive him, and she forgot to breathe. She could feel the lurch and skip of her heart and then the light tripping rhythm, and she had not expected this. She thought she had been prepared for it but she was not . . . she had never expected anything like this.

There was gentleness in his kiss, yes, but also intent, a purpose that paced further exploration and would not be denied. Dusty could sense this and it made her heart leap and then pound painfully even as her senses opened and clenched with helpless anticipation. She kept her hands closed tightly against his chest, trying desperately to control the urge to touch him and to hold him as he was holding her, trying not to offer him any encouragement. But in the end reason lost to instinct and one arm moved around his neck, the other hand opened to explore the tight muscled forearm below the sleeve of his T-shirt. His skin felt like satin, his hair like silk. Her mouth opened beneath his and his tongue slipped inside.

Camp made a low sound of pleasure in his throat, but the roar of her pulses all but obscured it. The taste of him, the feel of him filled her, touching nerves and drawing responses she had never dreamed she possessed before. Every part of her body seemed to pulse in rhythm to his, straining to blend with his, becoming a part of him everywhere he touched. When he gently withdrew his tongue and closed her lips with a touch of his own there was a bereft feeling, but it was quickly obscured by the electric heat of lips that moved slowly and deliberately over her face and at last culminated in the hot sense-stripping pressure of teeth and tongue upon her earlobe.

Camp had shifted his weight so that Dusty was lying upon her back beneath him, his chest a warm pressure against her breasts and his pelvis hard and urgent against hers. His breath was light and unsteady over her face as his tongue trailed a burning path downward to her neck and his hands slipped easily and smoothly beneath her T-shirt.

Then reason returned and she knew she should

stop it. But her breath was choked in her throat and the stifled sound of protest she made was easily stilled by his whispered, "Hush," and the closing of his lips upon hers. Just before she lost herself to the power of his kiss she caught a glimpse of his eyes. They were very bright blue, alight with pleasure and hazy with desire, they had the power to mesmerize her into a false sense of security and drown her with her own need.

His hands moved upward, brushing aside the material of her shirt, strong fingers cupping and gathering her breasts while his mouth inhaled her breath and his tongue captured and stilled her protest. But whatever protest she might have made was instinctual, not willing. Her limbs were numb and tingling, stripped of life and movement, her heart was a runaway organ of pumping dizziness, her entire body seemed to be no more than a receptacle geared to electric sensation.

With a soft intake of breath he moved over her, he buried his face in the mouth of her breasts his hands had created. Dusty's arms were about his neck, her fingers closing around rich handfuls of hair, her face averted and her lips parted in rapt attentiveness and aching need. And then nothing existed for her, nothing mattered, except the sensation of his tongue upon electrified flesh, the delicate probing explorations, and the deliberate sucking and drawing motions that sent a cascade of fire shivering down her abdomen and flowering in her loins. Pulsing flesh begged to be soothed by him and she ached for fulfillment of the emptiness he was carving so wonderfully and skillfully. Dusty wanted Camp. More than the physical satiation to her agonizing need, she wanted *him*, she wanted Camp, for he was the only one who would ever make her feel complete...

He shifted his weight again, his attention was concentrated with growing urgency on one throbbing breast while his hand trailed a burning downward course over her chest and her stomach, exploring and kneading the soft flesh of her abdomen. Warm rough fingers found the open snap of her jeans and slowly, inexorably, insinuated themselves beneath the tight waistband.

With a stifled sob, her fingers closed about his wrist. "Don't!" she whispered, choked. "Don't!"

Immediately responsive to her sudden panic, the stiffness that invaded each of her muscles and caused an instinctive shrinking away, he stopped. He lifted his face, his fingers moved to interlace with hers. His breathing was unsteady. "It's all right," he soothed huskily. His eyes were bright and passion-hazed, she wondered in that moment whether he even saw her. "Take it easy..." Why should that phrase, the sensuous tenor of his voice, only make her heart beat faster and her stomach start to clench in upon itself again? He soothed her as one would an overstimulated animal, with confidence and practiced skill. "It's all right," he repeated, and his hand moved to her face, drawing it toward him. "I won't hurt you..."

But he would. Not meaning to perhaps, but not caring that he did, he would hurt her. She wanted him, but he only wanted a woman. He needed release and she was convenient and after tomorrow he wouldn't even remember her name. "No!" It was a hoarse half sob and she braced her hand against his shoulder to push at him, rolling away from him and sitting up.

For a moment there was an awful flare of tension that seemed to shake the atmosphere around them, it scared her because she could almost feel rough hands grabbing her and dragging her down again. But it lasted for no more than a second, and then she could sense him forcefully bring his temper under control, she could feel him commanding his muscles to relax and his breathing to steady.

Her hands were shaking as she lowered the T-shirt to cover her breasts, and then she had to draw her knees up to her chin and hug them tightly because her whole body was shaking too. She sat drawn up in a little ball with her back to him, and there was a long, long time of nothing but aching misery and the sound of his breathing behind her.

And then he said quietly. "Why?"

Yes, why? Why had she stopped him when she knew she wanted him, when everything inside her still ached for him? He had brought something to life inside her and she had cruelly killed it...why was she punishing herself? But more than that, she was punishing him. She had teased him with her uncontrollable response, and that was cruel and uncalled for. After all he had done for her, he had a right to expect her to be accommodating...

Camp touched her shoulder lightly. "What happened, Dusty?" he insisted. His breath still sounded slightly uneven. "What's wrong, honey?"

"I am not your 'honey'!" Everything within her snapped and she whirled on him wildly, her voice hoarse and shaking, her eyes snapping. "I'm nothing to you but a quick tumble who happens to be in the right place at the right time! If you're in such bad shape you could have had it from that waitress last night—you didn't have to use me! I told you I'm not going to pay—"

His face was suffused with a dull color, the gentleness that had once been there was quickly replaced with tight fury, and his own eyes were dark and churning. "Damn it, I didn't *want* that waitress!" he exploded at her. "For heaven's sake, woman, didn't it ever occur to you that a man might want to make love to you because you're *you*—not just because you're convenient?"

For a time everything was suspended, the anger, the tension, the pulsing need and frustrated intentions, even the echoing of his voice inside the small confines of the truck. And she stared at him, wanting to believe it, aching to believe it, weakened by confusion and frightened by the anger on his face... Then that anger changed to disgust, his eyes skimmed away from hers. "Ah, hell," he growled tightly. "Forget it."

He flung himself over onto his back, his hand splayed across his chest, his eyes fixed upon the ceiling. She could see the jerky rise and fall of the pulse in his abdomen, patches of dampness on the blue material of his T-shirt. Misery and self-hatred coiled within her and she buried her face in her knees again, wanting to creep away and hide, knowing she had no place to go.

A very long time passed, silence punctuated only by the sound of his breathing, which gradually grew more even, and by the dull, painful thump of her heart beating out a slow pattern of emptiness. And then he said, much more calmly than before, "I said forget it." His fingers closed about her wrist and tugged gently. She looked at him. His eyes were calm, his face expressionless. "It's okay." She thought he meant it. "Let's get some sleep."

She hesitated, and his eyes met hers evenly, without any emotion at all—not kindness, not anger, not forgiveness, not desire . . . just nothing. She knew he would not touch her again tonight. She lay down beside him, careful distance between them, and he turned off the light.

She knew he did not sleep, any more than she did. The impenetrable darkness was the cloud that separated them, the stillness a buffer against pain. The sound of his voice made her tense again, startled and alert and a little frightened, because it was tight and angry, laced with bitterness. He demanded, "That guy you ran away from in Vegas—were you in love with him?"

Something quivered and threatened to break

within her with that, and she bit her lip with the pain and an unexpected scalding of tears. Peter. She couldn't face that nightmare so soon on the heels of this one, she couldn't tell him about that...

She heard the rustle of movement as he turned his head towards hers, she could feel the piercing eyes boring through the darkness. His voice was tight with warning and brisk with command. "Tell me, Dusty."

She closed her eyes hard and refused to let the tears escape. Her mouth and nose were clogged with moisture and it was a long time before she could speak. Even then it was with the greatest of efforts. "I can't," she whispered, and her voice broke. "Not now..."

He was silent. After a time she heard him turn his head toward the ceiling again, and the night lay still and oppressive about them.

It was a very, very long time later that he began to speak. "Our house was on the Common," he said softly, "a big brick two-story with white Doric columns and a brass knocker on the front door shaped like a lion's head. There was a huge oak in the front yard that must have been two hundred years old. One of the branches grew right up to my bedroom window and I used to climb out at night..."

Dusty closed her eyes and let one hot tear trickle down her temple as the sound of his voice fell over her like poetry, soothing and caressing, filling her most secret need with instinctive generosity, giving her the most precious gift—a part of himself.

Looking back, Dusty thought that was when she first began to love him.

Chapter Seven

Tension between them built like a steadily over-loading electric circuit the next morning. It was inevitable and perfectly understandable, yet that did not make it any easier to deal with on either of their parts. The end of the journey was in sight and the unresolved conflicts of the night before pressed against Dusty's back, the fear of the future was crowding in on her like a chore left too long undone.

Long after his voice had trailed away last night Dusty lay in wakefulness, treasuring what he had given her, holding back tears of gratitude and pathos. He did not sleep either, but lay in still wakefulness beside her, his voice tired and his mind full of what she had forced him to remember, either not knowing what else to say or not wanting to go on. And she reviewed each memory, each image he had drawn for her with aching wonder. She did not feel anything then but the need to hold him, to lie wrapped in his arms and sheltered by his warmth, and to sleep that way through the night. But she lay stiff and quiet beside him, careful not to touch him, and when at last the heavy wings of sleep carried her away it was into a fitful land of uneasy nightmares. Periodically she jerked into wakefulness to find only the smothering darkness of the truck and Camp beside her, still and silent, but awake.

They each welcomed the end of the night with puffy eyes and headachy fatigue which they tried to hide from each other. At first they were unbearably polite. He inquired whether she would like to go out for breakfast, she smiled falsely and told him she wasn't hungry. He asked if the air-conditioning was high enough, she told him it was fine. She asked if he would like her to read to him, he told her thanks, but not this morning. And when they couldn't keep it up any longer, they were silent.

But the silence only underscored the tension that tightened between them. It was just as well, Dusty kept telling herself, just as well their traveling days were almost over, because it was obvious they couldn't go on much longer like this. She was a burden and an inconvenience to him and he— well, he was simply driving her crazy with that incessant country music and the manic schedule he was keeping, not to mention what he did to her nerves every time he looked at her. She had enough problems, what with swallowing back motion sickness and constantly repressing the urge to bang in the stereo speakers with her fist, she assured herself, without worrying about trying to

GET THIS BOOK FREE!

MAIL TO:
Harlequin Reader Service
2504 W. Southern Avenue,
Tempe, AZ 85282

YES! I want to discover *Harlequin American Romance*.
Send me FREE and without obligation, "Twice in a Lifetime."
If you do not hear from me after I have examined my FREE
book, please send me the 4 new *Harlequin American Romance*
novels each month as soon as they come off the presses. I
understand that I will be billed only $2.25 per book (total
$9.00). There are no shipping or handling charges. There
is no minimum number of books that I have to purchase.
In fact, I may cancel this arrangement at any time. "Twice
in a Lifetime" is mine to keep as a FREE gift, even if I do
not buy any additional books.   154 CIA NAX7

Name	(please print)	

Address		Apt. No.

City	State/Prov.	Zip/Postal Code

Signature (If under 18, parent or guardian must sign.)

This offer is limited to one order per household and not valid to current
Harlequin American Romance subscribers. We reserve the right to
exercise discretion in granting membership. If price changes are
necessary, you will be notified. Offer expires February 28, 1985.

PRINTED IN U.S.A.

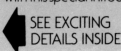

Experience *Harlequin American Romance*™...

with this special introductory FREE book offer.

◀ SEE EXCITING DETAILS INSIDE

Send no money. Mail this card and receive this new, full-length *Harlequin American Romance* novel absolutely FREE.

fight off his advances. She kept telling herself that, but she did not feel much better.

When he put the Eagles tape into the deck for what must have been the fiftieth time in forty-eight hours, she simply couldn't take it any longer. She inquired with as much evenness and forebearance as possible under the circumstances, "Don't you have anything by Neil Diamond or Barbra Streisand?" When a glance was her only reply, she specified sarcastically, "Don't you have anything that's *not* about life on the road, or the love of a good woman?"

He gave her one long look, then deliberately and rather childishly turned the volume up.

It wasn't too much longer before he said tightly, "Lady, if you snap that gum one more time I'm going to stick it to the tip of your nose."

She glared at him. "It's either chew gum or throw up all over the front seat of your precious rig."

His silence exhibited the great amount of control he was exercising over his temper. "I would prefer," he said at last, coldly, "that you do neither."

Yes, it was a good thing they were momentarily to part ways. Another day of forced confinement together and one or both of them would most likely end up victim of some violent crime.

When they passed a sign predicting the imminent approach of the Santa Fe City Limits, Dusty quietly reached in back and retrieved her cactus. She tried not to think of anything but how glad she would be to get out of the truck and on her own two legs again. *On her own.* Yes, that's what she needed to be. That's what she should have been all along. She would do much better with no one to worry about but herself, and so would he. She would have been better off had he left her alone, then she could have spent the last two days planning what she was going to do and starting to get her life back together, instead of growing complacent and soft and becoming used to being taken care of.

They were stopped at a red light when Dusty noticed a sprawling shopping mall on the right, a sure sign of encroaching civilization. Her voice was surprisingly tight as she said, "How much further to your delivery point?"

"Just a few miles." His voice, too, was tight, and he did not look at her. "Not far."

She spoke quickly, her voice as controlled and carefully polite as she could make it. "Then would you mind—if it's not too much trouble—just letting me off here?"

His glance was startled, almost taken aback. "What for? I told you—"

"Because I'd rather be stuck in a shopping mall with telephones and restrooms than in a warehouse parking lot," she snapped at him impatiently. "And if it's too much trouble for you to pull this rig into the mall I'll just get out on the street."

She reached for the door handle, but he swore softly and signalled a right turn.

It was early morning, the stores were just beginning to open, and the parking lot was not crowded. Camp pulled into an empty row near the front entrance and turned to her.

Dusty knew she should thank him. She tried to find some light and nonchalant way to say goodbye but suddenly the last thing she felt was nonchalance. Suddenly she realized this was it, she would never see him again, and why should her palms grow sweaty and a cold lump form in her stomach that felt like the beginning of a sob? She had known this moment was coming, from the beginning they had been moving toward nothing else. She was scared. She was alone and broke and she didn't know what was going to happen to her but of all those things the one that scared her the most was the thought of not seeing Camp again.

She turned to him uncertainly, and the look in his eyes took all her hurting and helpless motions and twisted them into anger. It was derisive, mocking, and impatient. And he said sarcastically, "All right, little Miss Independence, just what do you think you're going to do now?"

She couldn't stand it any longer, looking at him and feeling like she was going to cry, looking outside and seeing a strange and alien world fraught with unknown dangers. She fumbled with the door handle and retorted sharply, "I'm going to get out of this damn truck at last, thank goodness! And believe me, whatever I decide to do from here can't possibly be as bad as what I've been doing for the last two days!"

He grabbed her arm after exhaling a sharp breath. When she whirled on him, nostrils flared and eyes glittering, he seemed to reconsider whatever hasty words he had been about to utter. An expression of tight control came over his face and he said in an almost reasonable tone, "Look, this is stupid. I can't let you off here in the middle of nowhere—"

"The middle of nowhere is exactly where you found me," she returned coolly. "Please let go of my arm."

He did not. His temper was mounting. "Look, if you'll just come with me to drop off this load we'll see what we can do about getting you settled in somewhere—"

Every instinct within her rebelled at that. Dusty could not take more kindness from him, she would not let him insinuate himself into her life only to disappear from it without a backward glance as soon as she became dependent on him... She jerked her arm away. Her eyes were as hard as glass, and concealing the pain within her that was like a slowly twisting knife. "No, thank you very much, Mr. Campbell," she said coldly. "I prefer to take care of myself."

His eyes widened with disbelief and then swiftly narrowed with anger. "By God," he said slowly, "you really mean that, don't you?"

"Yes," she said coldly. Her voice was made expressionless by the enormous effort it took not to cry. "I've been taking care of myself long before you came along and I'll be taking care of myself long after you're gone. And"—she added with a defiant tilt of her chin—"I like it that way."

He stared at her for one more incredulous, soul-stabbing moment, and then the anger in his eyes began to twist into something suspiciously like concern. He demanded, "What are you going to do?"

"It's none of your business what I'm going to do!" she shouted at him, very near to losing control. "It has nothing to do with you at all!" Was he going to draw every last bit of pain out of this goodbye? Would he only be satisfied when he saw her melt into a sobbing puddle of helplessness at his feet? No, that she would not do, she swore determinedly to herself. That she would never do. With a short breath that was meant to be calming, she continued, "Do you think this is the first time I've ever been in this position?" She tried to keep her voice even. "Do you think this is the first time I've ever been broke and alone? Well, let me tell you, buddy, it's not by a long shot! I grew up fighting alley cats and winos for a place to spend the night and I made it this far—I've always made it, on my own! I sure as hell don't need some preppy cowboy telling me how to manage my life at this late date!"

She reached for the door handle again and Camp said coolly behind her, "Your Bronx is showing again, Love. I suggest you improve your dialect before you go on any luncheon interviews with the three-piece business suit type."

Her hand was shaking so badly she could hardly

get the door open, but she managed it. Just as she was about to spring to the ground he caught her arm again. She turned on him with a glare that could have killed.

He dug into his pocket for his wallet, and swore softly when he saw what was inside. In his eyes was a look of impatience and perhaps a tingling of regret for the harsh words that had gone before. "Look," he said, drawing out two bills. "All I have right now is twenty-five dollars. If you'll just come with me—"

"No!" She recoiled from the money he held out to her as though it were a poisonous snake. Her voice was a little hoarse, her eyes wide. "I don't want your money!"

"Why the hell not?" His patience was near the breaking point. "It's not much, but it's at least enough for you to eat on—"

"No!" She whirled blindly for the door. "I didn't do anything to earn it and I won't take it—"

"Will you stop thinking in terms of credits and debits?" Camp grabbed her shoulder and twisted her around in one ungentle movement. His face was taut with rage and impotence and his eyes dark. He shoved the bills down the front of her shirt and hard insensitive fingers probed carelessly at her breasts. In the same motion Dusty retrieved the bills and flung them back at him, tumbling clumsily out of the truck before he could grab her again.

"I don't want anything from you!" she screamed back up at him. Her face was mottled and her eyes glittering with sparks that could have been tears or fire. She was shaking all over. She only wanted him to go, to get out of her life and quickly so she could start forgetting about him. "I don't need anything from you—just leave me alone!"

He leaned forward on the seat, his own color darkening as the muscles in his jaw grew tight. His eyes were midnight blue and spitting sparks, and he made no effort at all to control his voice this time. He shouted at her just as she had shouted at him, viciously and spitefully, in a tone laced with contempt. "You think you're so damn smart! The tough little street kid who can lick the world with one hand tied behind her back! Well, let me tell you something, Dusty MacLeod—you're a child! An ignorant, helpless, immature child and your worst handicap is that you don't realize it. You're so smart you set off on a two-hundred-mile trek into the desert in high heels and a cocktail dress," he scoffed bitterly. "You're so smart you almost let yourself get raped by a gang of thugs and then you turn on the guy who tries to help you. You're so damn smart you turn up your nose at an honest offer of help when you've got no place else to go—ah, the hell with you!" He drew a sharp, violent breath. His eyes narrowed dangerously. "You're like a baby kitten hissing at a bulldog ten times its size, who doesn't have the sense to turn and run, and you won't even know what happened when you're eaten alive. I'll be damned if I'll be responsible for you," he swore at her. "You want independence—have at it! A man would be a fool to want a hellcat like you on his hands!" He slid behind the wheel and slammed the door violently. He left her with the sound of gears being shoved roughly into place and the Eagles once again blaring in her ears.

For a time she simply stood there, shivering in the desert sun, gulping back a sudden rising wave of despair and fighting the urge to cry. He was gone, and with him her anger, her defenses, even, for a time, her fear. He was gone and she felt empty. Nothing that lay ahead of her could be worse than that.

Santa Fe was a strange town, and no one looked twice at a girl wearing man's jeans and an overly large "I love Beethoven" shirt who wandered the mall holding a paper cup filled with sand. For a time that was all Dusty did. Walking, being on the move under the power of her own two legs, was therapy for her, a way of building courage, a feeling of being in control and doing something positive. There was no point in looking back. No point at all. It was not as though she had ever had a choice, it was not as though there were anything she could have done differently...The pain she was feeling now, if pain it was, had been predestined from the moment they met.

What had happened? How had a ride, a simple offer of assistance, turned into such a traumatic experience? How had she let herself get so involved with a stranger in only two days? She had let herself become dependent on him, just as she had with Peter...She had depended on Peter to the point of letting him strip her bare and destroy her life. What a fool she was! Wouldn't she have learned by now that self-reliance was the only thing she could rely upon? How could she go from one catastrophe straight into the arms of a stranger . . .

She had almost given herself to him last night. Dusty shuddered to recall her near escape. She had wanted him last night, and she loathed herself because even now her mind's eye kept flickering across the memory of muscled forearms and tufted chest, because she could feel the soft touch of calloused hands and the electric impulse of lips on hers and she knew no man had ever made her feel that way before . . . she was afraid no man ever would again. Yet if things had been different last night, nothing would be changed today. That she knew for a certainty. He had started something within her that was special and brilliant, it had the terrifying power to change her life . . . but for him it was only a matter of need, and convenience. If she had given in to her weakness and longing last night she would have had one night of ecstasy to measure the rest of her life by . . . and today she would still have been sitting alone and broken, in a strange desert town with nowhere to turn, and nothing but bittersweet memories in exchange for her heart.

No, she decided firmly, swallowing back the hot lump in her throat for the last time. She had done the right thing. She had done the only thing. Camp was gone, and it was right, it was only expected. He had given her a ride, a pair of hand-sewn moccasins, and a cactus in a paper cup ... and for that she would never forget him. But it was over now and she would not look back again.

Dusty sat on one of the stone benches strategically arranged near a waterfall in the airconditioned mall and tried to think what to do next. She was hungry. She berated herself for not accepting breakfast when Camp had offered it this morning, but she did not feel one moment's regret about refusing the money. That was simply beyond question. The important thing now was where did she go from here?

Of first priority was a job. A job meant money, it meant food, shelter, and—she looked down disparagingly at the ill-fitting jeans and top—clothing. Who would hire a vagabond like her? How could she walk into a plush personnel office looking like this ... with no permanent address, no telephone number, no references ... ? What did happen to someone cast adrift in a strange town with neither a change of clothes nor even identification ... She was a nonentity, an insignificant bit of flotsam on the tidal wave of humanity ... no one cared what became of her.

A momentary wave of panic swept over her but Dusty quelled it deliberately. She had been in worse shape before ... hadn't she? Surely she had. She knew what it was like to sleep in bus stations and on park benches, she had developed, to a science, the art of fending off offers of shelter from suspicious looking members of both sexes.

She knew how to lift an apple off a street stand
without ever arousing suspicion; she knew cons
that would make Oliver Twist proud...but she
had been a kid then. It had been almost a game to
her. And besides, she had never really been alone.
They traveled in gangs and she always had her
grandmother to go back to when things got really
tough. Dusty looked back on those days of her
turbulent adolescence and it was as though she
were seeing a life that belonged to someone else.
Oh no, she thought in sudden, almost paralyzing
despair, *I worked so hard to get away from there...*
And here she was right back where she had
started, a nameless street-orphan of twenty-six
with no money, nowhere to go, and no one to
turn to. Only, in many ways it was worse now. It
was worse because she had fought tooth and nail
to get away from the gutters that had turned the
companions of her youth into criminals, junkies,
and prostitutes; half of them dead before they
were twenty and the other half spending their
lives in and out of federal prisons. She had sworn
that would never happen to her, through sheer
determination and will she had taken the scraps of
heredity and environment and molded a life for
herself, a real life, with promise. It was worse because she had made it, she had had her hands
around the goal she had given her life's blood to
achieve—and she had lost it. Through her own
foolishness and weakness she had lost all she had
dedicated her life to. It was worse because this was
the adult world now; this was not a ghetto of New

York City where no one paid much attention to a gang of street kids, staying alive the best way they could. In the adult world survival did not come without sacrifice and sometimes that sacrifice was more than survival was worth. In the adult world a female with nothing but the clothes on her back—and even those did not belong to her—found herself with very few options. In the adult world the destitute and the broken sooner or later found themselves in the hands of slick looking men with white suits and feathered Panama hats, looking at dirty needles and learning not to complain about broken bones... if they wanted to survive.

It was worse because Dusty had been there, she had made it out; she had had all she had determined for herself and nothing less would ever do again. The world belonged to the rich and the middle class, she had been a fool to ever try for anything better for herself. Didn't her present situation prove it?

No. With one determined breath, a visible squaring of her shoulders, she refused to accept that. She couldn't give up now. *Now* was the worst time to give up. Dusty had made it before, she would make it again. And without the help of Mr. Leon Campbell, without the help of anyone. He had said she was helpless. He had said she was a child. What could a pampered Harvard boy playing at real life know about the desperation and panic that had driven her from a Las Vegas hotel into the desert with nothing but an overnight bag and fifty dollars in her purse? Hell, if *he* were mugged, all he would have to do is call up his rich family and his problems would be over as fast as the wire services could run. All right, so she had done a foolish and rash thing, but what did he know about the sudden mind-searing terror that blanked out reason when you saw your whole life ripped away and scattered like confetti on the wind? Camp had looked into her eyes and he had seen innocence there, he had seen straight through the tough facade and into her vulnerability . . . how had he done that? And how had he been able to see so clearly what Dusty tried so hard to hide, and then take it and twist it into a sign of weakness, of help-lessness? She was not helpless. She could make it here in Santa Fe just as she had long ago in New York, she would pull herself up by her own boot-straps if she had to. She would survive.

But Dusty was not a complete fool. Determina-tion had to be mitigated by reality, and she did not get her hopes up too much for immediate success. She knew before she tried what the reaction of the Director at the mall's second floor personnel ser-vice suite would be, but she dutifully filled out the forms with many blank spaces and tried to return skeptical looks with a confident smile. Next she made the rounds of individual stores, and she was not surprised that no one was interested. She did not let that dent her confidence. What did she ex-pect, dressed the way she was, looking the way she did? Obviously, she had to make some plans for the night, and then try again.

Where did the homeless and the destitute of

the world go? All was not lost; there were agencies equipped to deal with this sort of thing. One of the first things she should do, she realized as she searched through the Yellow Pages under "Charitable Organizations" was report her driver's licence and her Social Security card stolen—both symbols of identity and worth, and somehow, security. One could whip out a laminated card and say to the world, "Here, this is who I am, I am recognized by the United States Government as this number right here and I am worthy of your notice." The loss suffered by the absence of either of those two numbers was more psychological than physical.

Of course, Dusty did not have a dime to call for help, but she had the address of the nearest Salvation Army and the front of the telephone book obligingly furnished a street map, and she thought she could find her way. Dusty's last thought before she left the comfort of the air-conditioned mall for the desert sun once again was, *I never thought I'd be a charity case...*

Immediately she wished she had left her walking for a cooler time of day. July in New Mexico was not very hospitable to visitors. The sun broiled her scalp and painted spots of dizziness before her eyes and she thought the last thing she needed was to collapse of heat stroke on the side of the road. But she knew she had a long way to travel on foot and she did not particularly want to be on the streets of the city after dark, so she trudged determinedly on, staying to the main thoroughfares, looking purposefully as though she knew exactly where she was going and had every right to be here.

Dusty heard the approach of the big rig before she saw it. She did not know how she could be so sure it was the same one, but she was, just as she was sure, without looking up, that he would not stop. Why should he? His obligation to her was finished, and he had made it clear this morning that he had no more desire to continue their association than she had. He had schedules to keep and he had already done more than his share for the underprivileged of the world by taking her this far. Besides, she didn't need him, the last thing she wanted was more of his "help." And her heart was pounding dryly in her throat as she saw him signal a few hundred yards up the road and pull over onto the shoulder.

Dusty proceeded at a steady pace. The sun pounded in her head and every step on the gravelly shoulder jarred her bones. She tried not to think about what she would say to him, she tried not to wonder what had prompted his last-minute decision to pull over. It did not occur to her to wonder why, if he had had a delivery to make this morning on the other side of town, he was now on this side of the road, headed in the direction from which he had come. It simply did not occur to her that he might have come looking for her.

The rig looked wonderfully and unpredictably familiar to her. She squelched that reaction and kept her expression cool as she drew up beside the driver's door, her chin tilted up and her eyes expressionless as she looked at him.

Camp was leaning on the window, looking down at her. The sudden clenching in her chest was no more than relief at seeing a familiar face—it was amazing, how the human soul could hunger for a familiar face—and she carefully disguised even that reaction from him. His expression too, was carefully reserved, as though he was forcefully trying to put the harsh words of their parting out of memory and measuring his next words carefully lest they stir old anger in either of them. At last he said, noncommittally, "How's it going?"

"Okay." Her voice was just as unrevealing. "How about you?"

He squinted into the sun. "I'm dead-heading it to Pennsylvania. I've got two weeks to make it, though, so it'll be an easy trip."

She said nothing. Traffic whooshed by. His eyes wandered down to the cactus she still carried and something softened in his face, then quickly hardened. Willie Nelson began to croon a haunting misty-eyed melody and he abruptly clicked the stereo off.

His eyes skimmed over her face again, then toward the passing traffic. He began uncomfortably, "Look, Dusty, I can't just leave you here..."

Warning signals began to flash, but she did not know what they were warning against. Was there more danger in turning down this, his last offer of help, or in accepting it? Or were they simply two different kinds of danger—the one physical, the other potentially much more devastating. Her heart was pounding against her ribs. She said callously, "Don't do me any favors, cowboy. If I had to listen to one more whine from that stereo I think I would have screamed, not to mention what the smell of diesel was doing to my stomach. I wouldn't get back in that truck if you paid me."

"It's no barrel of fun traveling with a gum-chewing, smart-mouth teeny-bopper either," he shot back, scowling. His narrowing gaze fastened on her, penetrating. Camp demanded lowly, "Is this what you want?"

Dusty could not hold that gaze for more than a moment. Everything within her clamored, *No, it's not what you want. You know it's not! You want to be with him, to go with him to Pennsylvania or Transylvania or the ends of the earth for that matter. You want to let him make you feel special and cared for and secure, you want to feel his arms around you, protecting you . . . You want to be with him!* It pummeled her and shook her and took her by surprise and she knew then what the danger was. She couldn't. She could not accept even a ride from him, she could not risk getting back into that truck again . . . she could not risk growing dependent on him and trusting him in the same way she had trusted Peter. She was a fool to even consider it. She had to be on her own, she had to start

pulling her life back together and she had to do it
by herself, or two weeks from now she would only
be playing this same scene over again, nothing settled, nothing better, with nothing but a broken
heart and more crushed illusions to add to her
problems.

Stiffly, without looking at him, she nodded.

Abruptly, the muscles in his jaw clenched, his
eyes darkened. He reached for the gear shift. "All
right," he said tightly. "It's a free country. You're
over twenty-one. Suit yourself."

The truck rolled away from her at a snail's pace
and it seemed as though hope itself followed in its
wake. She stood there looking after it and fought
the urge to call out to him until every muscle in
her body quivered. Scalding tears blurred her
eyes. *Camp*, she thought desperately, helplessly.
Camp...

Brake lights flashed about two hundred feet up
the road. Dusty made herself start walking, her
legs were shaky and her body was clammy. She
firmly compressed her lips to keep them from
quivering. *Don't do this,* she told herself firmly.
You're crazy if you do this...

Once again he was looking down at her, one
strong brown arm resting on the open window.
His expression was enigmatic, and he simply
looked at her for a long time. She met his gaze this
time and let him read into it what he would—
stubbornness, pride, determination, and perhaps
if he looked far enough, need.

"Ah, hell," he said at last, wearily. "Get in."

With only another moment's hesitation, she walked around to the passenger door and got inside.

Chapter Eight

"Are you hungry?" He held out a bag of chocolate chip cookies to her.

Her stomach growled and she was glad he couldn't hear it over the throb of the engine. She shook her head.

He shrugged and took one for himself, setting the bag on the seat between them. She sat rigidly looking out the window, the cactus resting between her knees. What had she done? She had only set herself up for a bigger pain at the end of two weeks, and postponed dealing with her problems. Camp was addictive. Letting herself be taken care of was addictive. Nothing good could come of this, nothing.

After a time he said, "If it will make you feel better, you can earn your keep this time." Her head swiveled around to him and his lips curved tightly at her narrowing gaze. But he only said, "You can keep my log. It's worth taking on a passenger for that; lord knows I only make a mess of it myself."

How like him to immediately sense her need to clear herself of obligations and indebtedness. Gratitude spread through her in a softening wave. But she only said, staring relentlessly out the window, "You don't have to keep a log when you're not hauling."

She heard his sigh. "Look Dusty," he said after a moment, gently. "Everyone needs a helping hand now and then. It's nothing to be ashamed of. How do you think I got started out here on my own? I was just as lost and just as scared as you are, but someone took an interest in me and gave me a chance. It was the same when I wanted to finance this rig. Do you think anybody was going to loan me the money on my face alone? No, I had to have a backer, someone to give me a hand. I couldn't have made it alone."

She tossed her head with a derisive snort. "Spare me your sob stories of the struggling young lawyer-cum-trucker. All you had to do was crook your little finger and your family would come running. It's a little bit different for me."

"No," he said. Camp's voice was toneless. "My family didn't come running." Then he glanced at her. "The point is, kid, one of these days you've got to open up and give someone a chance to help you. This is the day," he finished decisively, "and I'm the someone."

Dusty stared at him. She couldn't prevent the incredulous question. "Why? What's in it for you? What—"

"Damn," he interrupted in a tight growl. "If

you say 'What am I going to have to pay' I swear I'll break every law in the book pulling this rig over so I can turn you over my knee.'' He shot her a dark glance that left no doubt whatsoever that his threat was serious. "And that's something that's a long time overdue, so keep it in mind the next time you think about giving me any back talk.'' Dusty's mouth snapped shut and he turned his eyes back to the road. It was a long time—a twenty count at least—before she saw the muscles of his arms begin to forcefully relax. Then he said, very calmly, "Nothing's in it for me—except you. You're worth it, that's all.''

She did not know how to take that; she dared not challenge him on it. She only knew that it made her feel good when he said that, warm and content and—yes, worth it. And it made her ashamed of herself. She looped her hands together in her lap and said lowly, "Camp...it's not just pride. Or if it is, it's because it's all I've got left. I've always had to make it on my own, I've always had to watch out for the sharks and the wolves and being suspicious is just another law of the jungle. Sometimes..." She cleared her throat a little against a sudden catch. "Sometimes I don't act too smart, I know. Sometimes I forget to watch out for the sharks and then—I pay. Like now. I just can't afford that.''

He was silent for a time, and she wondered what he was thinking. It was the closest she had ever come to telling him anything important about herself, she had at great risk lowered some of the barriers and made herself vulnerable to him, and he was silent. She expected an interrogation, and was surprised when all he said was, "Let's talk about your job prospects. What kind of experience do you have?"

She laughed a little without humor. "Name it. I've been a waitress, a theatre usher, a dishwasher... all kinds of things in between. There's not much I can't do."

"Are you a CPA?"

Dusty nodded proudly. "I have my degree."

"What about references?"

There she hesitated. Her voice sounded hollow when she said, "I worked for the same company for the past three years, but I don't think my boss is very likely to give me a reference."

He looked at her, and it was plain he knew the answer before he asked the question. There was a hard, blank look in his blue eyes. "Your boss wouldn't happen to be the man you left in Las Vegas?"

She nodded, and for some unknown reason felt a hot flush creep up her neck. She knew he was thinking all sorts of unsavory things, and some of them were probably true. Most of them were not, but she could not bring herself to offer a defense. She averted her face to look out the window.

He said, "I have a friend in Philly. A banker." His voice was emotionless. "I think he might be able to help you out with a job—if you're as qualified as you say you are."

She stared at him, for a moment breathless. "Do you—do you mean it?"

"Sure." His tone was casual, just as though he had not, with one careless movement, reached down and saved her life. "It only seems logical to me—accountants work in banks, don't they?"

Her head was spinning. She hardly dared to hope. "But—would he really take me in off the streets, with no references..."

He chuckled easily. "Honey, we've done each other so many favors over the years we've both lost count. So don't worry about that. You've got a job, if you want it, and if you can do it."

For another long moment she sat there, trying to absorb it. The sudden lifting of the crushing weight from her shoulders left her numb. Miracles did happen. All this time she had been certain her life was over, a second chance had been within arm's reach in the form of Camp...

"And here." He reached into his front pocket and presented her with a business card. "Just so you won't feel obligated to me—" He placed a slight derisive emphasis on the word. "Just in case you decide somewhere along the road that you can't stand the sight of me any longer and you'd rather try to make it East on your own—this is your insurance policy."

She took the card with the Philadelphia address and looked at it wonderingly. On the back was a hand-written note, "Bob—this is the woman I told you about. Give her a chance. Camp."

"You..." Her voice sounded choked. "You've

already talked to him? Before you even knew if I would come with you?"

She thought she saw the very faintest hint of color creep beneath his tan; he kept his eyes determinedly fixed on the road. "I didn't think you needed any more empty promises," he replied simply, offhandedly.

Suddenly Dusty was overcome with a sweeping urge to simply throw her arms around him and hug him. While that would certainly be the most effective method of expressing her emotions at that moment, she did not think he would appreciate the gesture under the circumstances, so she simply smiled at him. Her eyes were glowing. "Thank you," she said, very softly, somewhat tremulously.

The thank you was for more than the job, and when his eyes met hers, he knew it, and his own face softened in response. The gratitude was for his confidence in her, for his concern about her—but more, because in choosing this way to help her he had made certain she retained her independence. He had not used the promise of a job to bind her to him, he had understood that the only thing she would accept from him was that which was given freely, with no hidden provisos or strings attached. And in that gesture he had communicated to her more effectively than words ever could have done that she owed him nothing, now or ever, he had freed her from dependence on him.

He looked at her for only a few seconds—no more than the time he could afford to take his eyes off the road—but it seemed to Dusty a great deal was communicated between them in that time, and most of it had to do with a new level of understanding. For a second, just the briefest moment before he turned his eyes back to the road, she imagined she saw affection and tenderness in his eyes, and wonderful confusion started pumping in her chest at what she wanted to believe that look meant. When his eyes were straight ahead once again she ventured, somewhat shyly, "Do you—really have a load in Pennsylvania, or did you—come back to look for me, just for this?"

His scowl was somewhat false. "Of course I have a load. I'm not a complete idiot." But then the beginnings of a grin straightened out his frown and the glance he shot her was vaguely self-mocking. "The fact that it was in Pennsylvania was a bonus, that's all," he assured her innocently. And then his eyes were straight ahead, and he added very mildly, "Just don't ever look at me again like I'm an auctioneer at a white slavery market, and we should get along just fine, okay?"

Dusty felt a warm glow begin within her and spread slowly outward. She murmured, "Okay." Satisfied, he shoved a tape into the player. It was the sound track from the rock opera *Tommy*, and his quick glance dared her to challenge his compromise. She only smiled and reached for a cookie.

They stopped for lunch in a village that was charmingly Mexican, and Camp introduced her to the culinary experience of authentic tacos within a restaurant that featured wooden ceiling fans and bare oak tables. Dusty gorged herself, disregarding the promise of indigestion that would undoubtedly assail her as soon as she got back into the truck. Camp was in such a good mood, and she was feeling so wonderful about him and the world and life in general, it was difficult to worry about anything—from indigestion, to what would become of the sleeping arrangements in the wake of their frustrated intimacy last night.

Camp flung his arm companionably around her shoulders as they left the restaurant for the hot dusty glare of the New Mexico sun. "Do you know, this is like a vacation for me," he confessed. "I've been driving seven days a week for the past six months—sometimes straight through, and it will feel good to meander across the country at my own pace for a change. I'm going to take advantage of it, too. Would you believe," he said, "there is actually a park in this place, with real shade trees. I can't think of anything I'd rather do right now than take a nap in the open air under one of those trees. I didn't get too much sleep last night," he added, and the look in his eyes was an explicit reminder of the reason why. She quickly avoided his gaze.

Camp went back to the truck for a blanket, and Dusty purloined a paperback novel from his supply. The park he had mentioned was not much in the way of parks, but it was a pleasant surprise in this barren place, and largely unoccupied at midday. And it did have shade. The day was hot and still but the lack of humidity made it comfortable, and Dusty gradually felt herself begin to relax into pure and unthinking contentment.

Camp stretched out on the blanket and pulled his hat over his eyes; within moments he was asleep. Dusty opened the book and started to read, but repeatedly she found the appeal of Camp's strong, relaxed body beside her to be greater than that of the fictional plot before her. The sun threaded gold through the strands of hair that waved over his neck and bronzed his lightly hair-covered arms. The T-shirt clung to the muscular rise and fall of his chest and made her wonder how it would feel to have her head pillowed against that strong breast, and his arm circling her waist in warmth and security. But then she determinedly jerked her eyes back to the book. She must be crazy. Hadn't she learned her lesson? Didn't she know by now the consequences of becoming involved? She had only one thing to concentrate on now, and that was getting over the results of the last time she had listened to her heart and not her head. She could not afford to think about anyone but Dusty right now. And Camp... it was ridiculous. It was suicidal. In two weeks they would say a permanent goodbye—assuming they could manage to stay away from each other's throats for that long—and this would be no more than a brief interlude in the whole of their lives. Dusty found it strangely painful to think about saying that permanent goodbye, so she didn't. She devoted all her attention to unraveling the saga of the fictional Barret family as they pioneered the Midwest.

Time passed immeasurably as she turned page after page, and she did not know how long Camp had been awake, watching her. He said, "I haven't finished that book."

She glanced at him only briefly, for by now she was completely immersed in the story. She could only see one solution to the problem, and she read, "'I've never known a woman like you, Amy,' said Tyrone huskily. His eyes swept hungrily down—"

"Wait a minute." Camp turned over on his stomach, frowning. "What happened to Elizabeth?"

"She got raped and scalped by the Indians in chapter three," replied Dusty.

"What about their kid?"

"He was carried off by the war party."

"Who's Amy?"

"Elizabeth's sister from Virginia."

"Okay." He propped his chin on his fists and stared fixedly at her thigh. "Tell me some more about Tyrone's hungry eyes."

Dusty refused to be unnerved. She read the remainder of the passionate passage with such outrageous melodrama and inflection that Camp was soon convulsed with laughter. She was trying so hard not to laugh herself that it was impossible to turn the page, and she gave only one squeaking protest when he grabbed the book from her and tossed it aside, then captured her waist with his arms and dragged her down on the blanket beside him. His face was very close, blue eyes snapping with laughter, warm breath fanning her cheeks as he exclaimed, "You have a devilish streak in you, don't you Dusty MacLeod? Just like me." And the laughter gently faded from his eyes into something warmer as he brought his hand up to smooth back her hair. "A lot of things about you remind me of myself," he said softly. His eyes moved across her face in a leisurely, caressing way, and the pounding of Dusty's heart that had begun with the brief playful struggle abruptly changed to a light, rapid tripping. His arm around her waist was warmly pleasurable. The absent, tender motions of his hand upon her hair, mesmerizing. She wanted him to go on looking at her, and touching her, in exactly that way forever. "The stubbornness, the stupid pride, the headstrong impulses...we're two of a kind, Dusty."

With her partial weight resting on his chest and her elbow her only support, his face was only inches below her. It was a beautiful face, strong and kind and open, a face she could see becoming part of her life, a face she could too easily come to rely upon...

Her voice was a little husky, and somewhat breathless, as she replied, "That must be why we don't get along so well."

His lips curved into a lazy, purposeful smile. "Oh, we get along all right," he murmured, and his hand slid around to cup the back of her skull. "Sometimes..."

The pressure he exerted, if any at all, to lower her face to his, met with no resistance. Her lips met and parted for his with an instinct as natural as the rising of the sun and just as wonderful. This was where she belonged, in his arms with his lips sending electric sparks of pleasure through her, his hands molding her into helpless, delightful compliance against him, and passion and yearning swelling in powerful tides with every caress, every touch of his tongue or lips ... He had the power to evoke from her unimagined sensual depths, to blind her with her own response, to erase her mind of everything but the pleasure she found in his arms and her need for him. And that need was so powerful it was frightening. It stripped her body into a mindless vessel aching to receive him, it emptied her mind and fired her emotions to a wonderful, churning turmoil. Joy and pleasure, wanting and fear, aching, demanding need were all tangled up inside her and lost as his hands moved with tender leisure over the curve of her hip and traced the rounded pressure of her breast. Her erratic breathing became interlaced with his own as his lips moved across her face and his caresses commmunicated his own growing urgency. Weakness was generated from the touch of his hand and spun slowly outward and over her, and in his arms she was helpless. Helpless.

"Ah, Dusty," Camp sighed against her ear. The warmth of his breath sent a shiver over her and the gentle nibbling motions he made against her earlobe were maddening, paralyzing. There was tenderness in the way he held her but she could feel the urgency within him and knew that his restraint was exercised at great personal cost. "Let's go back to the truck. I want to spend the rest of the afternoon making love to you..."

She stiffened. She didn't want to but she made herself struggle out of his arms and his own swift hurt and anger were only another knife thrust to the pain that was stabbing through her. What was she doing? What was she thinking of? Why was she volunteering to walk through a door that opened only on pain and loss...She could not take any more pain. And this man had more power to hurt her than any she had ever known. More, even, than Peter...

She said thickly, getting clumsily to her feet, "We'd better get on the road. It's late."

His hand clamped around her wrist with steely strength, and, in a single movement, he jerked her beside him again. His face was dark with rage and tight with the effort to control it, his eyes were black slits. She was startled and frightened, even last night he had not been this angry, and this low rage terrified her not only with its unleashed power, but with the coldness and emptiness that flowed through her when she faced it. She did not want him to be angry with her, she wanted him to hold her and comfort her. But his fingers were like talons as they dug into tender flesh and crushed against fragile bones and he said lowly, "Not this time, lady. This time you're going to tell me."

Her eyes filled with silent agony, both emotional and physical, and he abruptly released her wrist. He turned in a short movement away from her, one fist clenched tightly against the blanket beside him as the other arm encircled a bended knee, every muscle in his body strained to control the volcano that was churning within him. Dusty could hear the sound of his short, harsh breaths that he struggled to bring under control and she was both terrified and sorry, so sorry to have done this to him ...

His voice was a controlled growl that echoed her own pain. "Do you have any idea what this is doing to me?" Another short, sharp breath. "Do you know how much I want you and how hard it is for me to keep my hands off you ..." And suddenly he jerked his head around to face her, his expression more a mixture of agony and fury than rage, felt like a physical blow, she actually shrank back beneath the force of it. "And damn it, I know you want me too!" His voice was still very low, very carefully controlled. His eyes were glittering magnets that both mesmerized with power and repelled with danger. "Why are you doing this? Don't you think I can see in your eyes that you hate it as much as I do? *Why*, Dusty?"

Her throat flooded and convulsed, she opened her mouth to speak but nothing came out. With her eyes she tried to tell him, but his own pain obscured his vision. And on her shaky breath the low violence within him erupted into a harsh demand, "Are you playing some kind of game with me? Is this the way you get what you want out of men?"

Utter horror compelled her to shake her head, and the gasp was torn from her throat, "No, I—"

"And don't give me any of that simpering crap about 'you only want my body'!" The bitter derision in his voice was sharp and wounding. "That's part of it, I won't deny it, but it's as much true for you as it is for me! And if that's all I wanted, don't you think I know I could have it?" Suddenly his fingers grasped her chin, hard and purposeful with contained strength, he turned her to face him and would not let her go. "You melt when I touch you, Dusty." Camp's voice was low and smooth, his eyes dangerous. She could not help shivering when those eyes went over her, powerful in their intent and all the more so for the quiet huskiness of his voice. His fingers dug into the soft skin of her chin and hurt; completely at odds with the lover-like tone of his voice. "I know just how to kiss you, just where to touch you... and I don't have to stop when you tell me to." The violent hunger in his eyes made her shiver again and she was pinned helplessly within their power by his fingers and his voice. "Especially..." And then he released his grip abruptly. "When I know you don't mean it. But I want more from you than just physical response, Dusty, I want more than the animal instinct—" And then he broke off with a breath; the curse he uttered as he turned sharply away from her was indistinguishable.

Dusty couldn't move. She wanted to get up and

run—away from his anger, from her own twisting and tearing emotions, away from the danger that pulsed and throbbed between them like a physical thing. But her legs were trembling, there was an emptiness in the pit of her stomach that generated outward weakness, and she could only sit there listening to the sound of his harsh breathing and staring at the tight muscles of his back, wanting to cry, wanting to hide, not knowing what to do.

It was a long time before he said, not looking at her, "I've tried to be gentle with you. It's not easy." His voice was forcefully calm, determinedly truthful. "I've tried not to frighten you even though you bring out a violence in me that's not easy to deal with. When I'm with you I can hardly think, I want you so much, but I try to hide it because I don't want you to think I'm just another man trying to use you..." He looked at her suddenly, and the raw emotion in his eyes was like a knife thrust between her ribs; she couldn't breathe. "When you left me this morning it was all I could do to keep from hauling you back into the truck and tying you down—I think if I could have gotten my hands on you, I would have wrung your neck. You make me crazy, Dusty, I don't know myself when I'm with you. You make me do things and feel things that I never thought I was capable of before. I hate what you do to me but damn it, I can't get you out of my head! You're not just another woman to me, you're—"

What? *What?* Every part of her screamed to know, she trembled with the effort to repress the yearning and her heart thundered painfully in her chest. But once again he averted his face, the muscles of his jaw tight and his lips compressed. She wanted to touch him so badly it hurt. She bit her lip and clenched her fists and waited for him to speak again.

When at last he did, his voice had regained its even tenor. He still did not trust himself to look at her. What was he afraid she would see in his eyes? More promises he had no hope of fulfilling, emotion he did not want her to share? "I've tried to teach you to trust me," he said, very steadily. "I've tried to show you that I care about you as a person, not just as a sexy body . . . I've tried to be honest with you. I didn't want to hurt you." His eyes, as they riveted on her face, were sharp and demanding. "Have I done that, Dusty?" he insisted. "Have you learned to trust me? Or am I fighting a losing battle?"

She licked her dry lips, her nostrils flaring with choppy breaths. His eyes followed the movement and she did not know whether she could speak. "Yes," she managed at last, hoarsely. "I—I know you're not like the rest . . ."

"Then what?" The demand in his voice was clear, even though his tone was gentle. The harsh lines on his face softened somewhat, making it easier to look at him. "Dusty, the attraction is mutual, you know it is. You're a grown woman, too old to be playing puritanical morality games. What are you defending yourself against? Why are you afraid of me?"

"I—I'm not afraid of you," she stammered, and she knew it was true. Not in the literal sense, at least. What she was afraid of was herself, and the power he had to make her want him, to want more than just a night or two in the back of a truck...the power he had to take from her all that she wanted when he left her.

"Dusty..." His voice was quiet. His fingers moved on the blanket and then stilled, as though he refused to let himself touch her. "You respect yourself enough to turn me down; I'm not holding that against you. But don't you respect me enough to tell me why?"

How could she refuse the sincere persuasion in his voice, in his eyes? She did not want to tell the truth for in doing so she would only make herself more vulnerable, yet how could she hold back more of herself from him when all she wanted to do forever was give to him and go on giving?

She raised helpless eyes to him, pleading for his understanding. "Camp—don't you see I can't—can't deal with this, now. It's a dead end, you and I—I don't want to be another name you can't remember on your list of one-night stands—"

"It's not just one night!" he interrupted harshly.

"Two weeks, then!" Her own control was beginning to break, cracking her voice and clawing at her anger. "Two weeks on the road between New Mexico and Pennsylvania, a good time was had by all, no commitment, no hang-ups, love 'em and leave 'em—"

"For heaven's sake, Dusty," he exploded at her, "what do you want from me? A marriage proposal?"

The moment seemed frozen for Dusty, the harsh impatience in his face and the ringing frustration in his voice faded out and left only the stunning truth echoing in its wake... Yes, that was what she wanted. She wanted to spend the rest of her life knowing and discovering him, living with him and letting him make her feel alive, she wanted strong arms sheltering her and quick, intelligent eyes seeing through her defenses and finding the worth there. She wanted the sound of his voice and his lopsided grin and his understanding silences. She wanted his passion inflaming her every night and the clean sleepy scent of him wafting over her every morning. How had this happened, how had it crept up on her, this insidious need for him; how had it, without her knowledge, implanted itself firmly within the heart of her and begun to demand permanence? It was impossible, it was incredulous, she did not have to look at his face to know that. But she did want him... forever.

When she focused on him again she caught just a moment of something odd on his face—confusion, uncertainty, and perhaps, even pain. But she did not have a chance to wonder whether that look had been caused by something he read on her face because he quickly dropped his eyes. He drew a breath, his voice was quiet when he looked at her again. "Dusty," he said simply, soberly, "there are all kinds of relationships. What's between us is more than just the mating urge, you know that. We have a relationship, a very special one, it's been building since I picked you up on that Nevada highway and I think you know it's beginning to mean something to both of us. It may not be based on permanence and..." Why did he stumble over the word? "...commitment, but two weeks is all we have, Dusty. That's more than a lot of people ever have. I don't want to spend that time fighting with you," he finished simply.

Sudden agony twisted inside her at the open sincerity in his face, the finality of his words. Why? she wanted to cry out loud. Why did it have to be that way? Why had she stumbled so unwillingly upon the one thing she had been looking for all her life only to find herself boxed into a self-imposed deadline, a now-or-never ultimatum? Why did it have to happen now and with him?

She looked at him, only to find her eyes suddenly and unexpectedly flooded with hot tears; she had to quickly lower them again. "Please..." she managed in a moment. Her voice was tight and threatened to crack. "Don't be angry with me."

He was silent for a long time. His profile was directed towards the sun, when she glanced at him she could see the lines and crinkles etched into his bronzed face but nothing else. He said at last, calmly, "I'm not angry." And then he turned to her; he took her hand and pulled her to her feet. His eyes were clear, but expressionless. His voice was a determined promise. "But don't expect me to stop trying," he said. "I can't do that, Dusty."

But he did stop trying, sooner than she had expected . . . sooner than she had wanted.

Chapter Nine

They stopped for the night at a rest area indistinguishable from all the others along the road, littered with cacti and wilting palm trees and a few scraggly patches of scrub grass that bravely fought for survival in the hostile sand. Camp had tried to disguise his moodiness from her during the afternoon, he tried to pretend nothing was amiss, and Dusty tried just as desperately to meet him halfway. But too often he fell into brooding silences; when he asked her to read to him she knew it was only because he did not want to try to keep up conversation with her, and that he was not hearing what she read. Over and over the dull truth pounded at the back of her skull. *This was a mistake, you knew it was a mistake, it will never work... We can't go on like this for two weeks.*

They had a generally silent dinner of sandwiches and potato chips, and Dusty was glad to escape to the restrooms for a sponge bath—there were no shower facilities—and a change of clothes. Camp was not at the truck when she returned; she found him at last, sitting near a clump of cactus some distance away from the activity of the parking area, drinking from a bottle, and watching the sunset.

· She started to turn back, certain he had sought privacy for a reason, but he smiled when he saw her and patted the sand beside him. "You know," he confessed when she sat beside him, "the desert can be damned beautiful at times. You don't get sunsets like this back East."

She looped her arms around her knees and nodded in silent agreement. The brilliant crimsons and vibrant blues were surrealistic brushstrokes across an electric sky, it was almost too beautiful to look at. She watched until it faded to an equally clear and definitive twilight—only a matter of a few moments—and then she turned to him. "What are you drinking?" she inquired casually.

He lifted the bottle to her. "Genuine mescal tequila, in celebration of our last night in New Mexico. Have you ever tried it?"

She shook her head, an endearing grin stole across his lips as he passed the bottle to her. "Then let me be the first to introduce you to a hangover you will never forget as long as you live. Now wait—there's a technique to this. First you put a little salt on the back of your hand..." She watched him skeptically as he poured a sprinkling of salt from the shaker on her wrist. "And then," he continued elaborately, his grin again twitching, "if we had a lime you'd take a bite out of it, but we don't so we'll skip that step... Now, real quick, lick the salt and take a shot of tequila— instant margarita.''

She licked the salt off the back of her hand but just as she was bringing the bottle to her lips she gasped, "Camp, there's something in the bottle!"

"Don't worry," he assured her complacently, "it's just a worm."

She shrieked and he caught the bottle before she dropped it. His shoulders were shaking with laughter. "Come on, honey, what's one little worm between friends?"

"Little!" She rubbed her lips, which had never touched the bottle, viciously. "It's as big as a snake! Ugh!" She shuddered dramatically. "How could you drink that stuff? Didn't you see it when you bought it? How disgusting!"

He doubled over with laughter, and she scowled at him, half in indignation for his reaction, half in horror of his hygiene habits. When he looked up, his eyes were snapping like capricious electric sparks. "You're priceless!" he exclaimed. And then, sobering a little, "Come on, Dusty, you don't mean to say a sophisticated young lady like yourself has never heard of the 'Legend of the Worm'?"

Her scowl deepened in confusion. "The what?"

He held the bottle up to the fading light and she shrank back in distaste. "This, my dear," he informed her dramatically, "is no ordinary garden variety worm. The creature spends its entire life growing and feeding on the mescal plant, and we all know what mescal is the origin of, don't we?''

"Mescaline?" she ventured, and he nodded approvingly.

"So," he continued in the same lecture-hall tone, "besides having one incredibly happy caterpillar embalmed within..." She giggled. "We also have a bottle of very expensive tequila, whose prime ingredient—the worm, is supposedly imbued with mystical powers. It is said that eating the worm..." She shuddered and, with an awful face, recoiled from him. He ignored her. "... will result in a religious experience, expanded consciousness, universal awareness—" He glanced at her. "In other words it will make you higher than the proverbial kite."

Dusty couldn't seem to erase that look of ultimate repulsion from her face. "Have you ever—?"

"Me? No. I've never been able to drink enough tequila to get up the courage. There are those, however, who are into that sort of thing, who claim that the worm is the key to a mystical experience unlike any they've ever known. Of course," he admitted, "looking at the bottom of the bottle of tequila, it wouldn't take too much to make you feel like flying."

She looked at the disgusting manifestation for a moment longer, wincing when he brought it to his lips again, "That's—weird," she ventured at last. "Do you suppose there's anything to it?"

Camp's eyes twinkled at her in the fading light.

"My dear, it is my considered opinion that these caterpillars are plucked off the back of some melon truck on the Texas border and shoved into the bottles just before they go through customs. However..." He shrugged. "It sells tequila. To each his own." He drank again.

"I can't watch this," Dusty murmured sickly, and started to rise.

He laughed and caught her hand. "All right, no more talk about worms. Pretend I'm drinking soda pop. You don't even have to look. Just keep me company."

A little reluctantly, she settled beside him again. She did not know why he wanted her to stay, but she really wasn't anxious to go back to the truck. The evening was pleasant, the sky soon a magnificent canopy of bas-relief stars on a crystal-black background, the air around them still and warm. They were silent, enjoying the beauty around them, Camp occasionally drinking from the bottle and Dusty trying not to think about it, eventually succeeding. She murmured at last, "It's nice out here." And her voice was drowsy with contentment, his monosyllabic agreement a lazy echo.

He picked up a stick and began to absently poke holes in the sand. Dusty felt something change about his mood, she had grown so sensitive to him that she could feel tension gathering in his muscles even when she could not see it. She glanced at him curiously, but he seemed lost in brooding thought, he did not speak for a time.

When he did, his voice was an odd tone, heavy yet strangely matter-of-fact. "Dusty," he said, "there's something I want to tell you."

Immediately her attention was attuned to him, alert and waiting and quickly receptive. He glanced at her, but his eyes were unrevealing. He looked back to the pattern of holes he was creating in the washed-out sand.

"Today," he began quietly, never once raising his eyes to her, "when I saw you walking along the road—and before that, when I found you on the desert highway—I saw a picture of my own life five years ago and it was so sharp, so clear, it actually felt like someone had punched me in the stomach. You see, when I first came out here I didn't have anything but the shirt on my back, I had done one rash and foolish thing, and my whole life came tumbling down around me. Everything that I knew, all that I had grown used to and had come to depend upon was gone in one fell swoop, like a domino house when you remove one block. And instead of turning around and trying to build again I walked away from it and tried to start over with a new life—eventually I walked so far and so long that it was too late to turn back and there wasn't much left to start over with. I burned my bridges behind me, Dusty, and I didn't want to see that happen to you—not while there was still a chance that you could make something out of the life you thought you'd lost."

Something warm and tentative clenched within

her, she tried with all her might to read something in the face that was shadowed with starlight. "What happened?" she insisted softly. "What did you leave behind?"

He made a short sound that resembled laughter, the hole he stabbed in the sand was particularly vicious. "It wasn't a matter of leaving it behind so much as it was running away." He took a breath, still not looking at her. "I told you I was always a hothead, a rebel. I didn't necessarily go looking for trouble, but I sure didn't mind when it found me. I had a rebellious streak and when that's combined with a crusading nature and a strong sense of idealism it can be explosive—especially in the courtroom." Another breath, and a clump of sand flew beneath the thrust of his stick. "I was six months past my bar exam and I thought I was the greatest thing the law had seen since Moses. Nothing got in the way of my relentless quest for truth, justice, and the American ideal. I got all the cases nobody else in the firm wanted—the losers, the derelicts, the no-wins and no-pays—I even took on a few against my father's will which, needless to say, did not make for a very good working relationship. We were always at each other's throats over my cases. He wanted me to be a part of the firm; I wanted to practice law." He shrugged, dismissing the anger that had momentarily tightened his voice.

"Anyway, there was this hardnosed judge—a hopeless alcoholic, a philanderer, a disgrace to his robes and completely incompetent to sit on the bench... Everyone knew it and it was kind of a joke around the law community. It infuriated me. The man was in the back pocket of every official from the mayor on down. Sometimes he came to court so drunk he couldn't even read the depositions. And they were making a mockery of what I considered a sacred institution, letting him rule, patronizing him, laughing about him at cocktail parties.... Well, eventually, it was my misfortune to try a case before him. It was a fiasco from the word go. Damn..." Here his voice tightened briefly. "He *slept* through most of the evidence. It's a long story, but in the end he sent my client to prison on a technicality—something that had nothing to do with his guilt or innocence, the evidence against him, or the lack of it... He sentenced a nineteen-year-old kid to three years in the state penitentiary when even the prosecutor knew he was innocent—all because some clerk in some office forgot to dot an *i* or cross a *t*." Camp's release of breath was long and calming. He let the stick fall slack in his hand. "Well," he finished flatly, "I lost it. I went crazy. I was cited for three charges of contempt before I finally dragged the bastard down and gave him what he deserved with my fist." His soft laugh was surprising, even though it was laced with bitterness. "I look back now and I can't believe I did that. I can't believe it was me, Leon Campbell from the long line of illustrious Campbell attorneys, who jumped on a judge in a courtroom like a kid in a schoolyard brawl. It seemed worth it at the time.

"Well, naturally, I got to see the inside of the county jail for the first time as something other than a visitor. There was a list of charges against me a mile long, some of them pretty accurate, some of them fabricated out of thin air. My father didn't even try to post bond; that didn't surprise me. By the time I managed to raise bail myself I had had plenty of time to think, and I realized what an idiot I had been—I was as ashamed of myself as he was of me, I was sure. But that didn't change the fact that I was right in principle if wrong in action and I did expect my father to see that, I hoped he would try to understand and that we could work from there. My license to practice law could be on the line, I knew that, and even though I had been wrong and I was ready to admit it, I needed my father's help to save my neck; I wasn't too proud to ask for it." There was a silence. "I went back to find my office cleared out and my name off the letterhead and my father wasn't in the office to me. When I finally managed to break through the army of secretaries and clerks there was such coldness in his eyes, such contempt... He looked at me as though I wasn't there, and then he went right back to dictating his letter and never once acknowledged my presence except to call the security guard to have me thrown out."

Now the silence seemed endless. Dusty's heart was breaking for him, she wanted to put her arms around him and hold and comfort him, but he was very far away from her, lost in his own memories and pain that nothing she could do or say would erase. And then Camp finished dully, "I guess something in me just snapped. That look in his eyes was the end of the last of my illusions, my hope that I could somehow one day fit in to his world and be what he wanted me to be. I didn't want to try any longer. So I just left. I skipped bail, I went to another side of the country, and I guess subconsciously I was trying to put as much distance between my old life and my new one as I could. I took the most physically trying jobs I could find—digging sewers, collecting trash, and eventually, driving a truck. I see now that I was trying to punish myself. I guess even when I went into independent long-hauling, somewhere in the back of my mind I was thinking about how it would make my father feel if he knew to what use I was putting my Harvard education..." The twist of his lips was self-mocking. "Stupid, isn't it?"

Dusty watched him bring the bottle up once again and drink deeply, grimacing as the liquid hit his throat. She watched his sharp profile in the pearly light and the movement of the shadows that made his face look suddenly vulnerable, and she was filled with love for him so complete, so overwhelming that for a time she couldn't speak. She could only sit there, knowing him, loving him, feeling a part of him for all he had shared with her and wanting him forever in her life.

He spoke at last, with forced negligence and a

quick, sideways glance at her. "At any rate, five years of this rough pioneer stuff has pretty much matured the spoiled brat in me. If I had it to do over again of course I'd do it differently, but..." He shrugged and drank again.

"Camp," she said softly, in a moment, "why don't you go back? Don't you ever look back on all you lost and think about it...don't you ever want to just settle down?"

"Oh, I think about it all right," he said quietly. "Especially since..." But he broke off and drank quickly from the bottle. "It's too late," he said curtly. "I wasted it all in one stupid, impulsive move, and there's nothing left to go back to. I skipped bail. There are still probably charges against me, and as for ever practicing law again..." He let that thought finish itself. "As for my father and what might be left of my family... There's just too much to face back there, Dusty." His voice was as barren and as bleak as the landscape surrounding them, speaking more eloquently than words of the depth of his loss. "And nothing worth facing it for."

She sat beside him in silence, everything within her wrapping itself around him and holding him, emotions too deep for words or even gestures. A moon rose over them that was so big and so bright it almost hurt the eyes, it washed the emptiness around them with gossamer daylight, it bathed them with warmth and caressed them with soft shadows. They sat there until time was little more than a memory, and were lost in the gentle sharing that wrapped them together with a stronger tie than any touch or embrace could do. And Dusty wanted nothing more than to be with him, like this, time without end.

The bottle was half empty when he said, "Now your turn. Tell me Dusty." When she hesitated, he gave her a small smile and assured her, "Don't worry, I'm so drunk I won't remember a word of it in the morning. You can trust me."

That she knew already. Even as it had been painful for him to revisit his past and relive the humiliation of youthful follies it would be even more so for her. She had so much more to be ashamed of. She did not want to keep secrets from him any longer, but she was afraid of losing his regard which had become so precious to her... She was afraid that, if he really knew her, he would no longer look at her in the same way.

And then she looked into his calm, clear blue eyes and she suddenly realized that he had wrestled with something of the same fear when he had made his confession. She could not refuse to share herself with him when he asked. She joked nervously, "This is the night for baring our souls, hmm?"

"In lieu of anything better," he agreed lightly, and the quick spark in his eyes had the immediate effect of easing the tension.

She shrugged and began her story. "I grew up more or less on the streets. My mother..." There was no easy way to say this. She looked down at her hands and forced it out. "My mother was a call girl. I never knew my father. My mother—for obvious reasons—didn't want me around a lot. Sometimes the men she brought home—would try to..." She heard his sharp breath, her glance revealed his brows drawn together in a tight, piercing frown. She looked away uncomfortably. "Well, it wasn't too smart having a little girl around, especially as I got older, so I spent a lot of time away from home. Mostly I lived with my grandmother, but she was—strange. She was always preaching to me about bad seeds and the sins of the fathers and—that wasn't much fun either. So I ran away a lot." Dusty ventured another glance at him, and even managed a small smile. His face was still drawn into that ominous scowl, his eyes were very hard. She managed a small, stiff smile. "Not exactly life at home with Ward and June Cleaver, was it?"

He focused on her. His eyes had a strange glitter to them and his voice sounded a little hoarse. "But you were just a little kid—and you had to watch your mother... Didn't anyone try to do anything about it?"

She shrugged. It had become so much an accepted part of her life that she rarely thought about it any more. "What could anyone do, even if they cared?"

"The men..." Now his voice sounded very strange, his eyes seemed to go right through her. "Did they hurt you?"

She shook her head. "It was just scary, sometimes. And confusing." She ran a nervous hand through her hair. "Oh, I suppose a psychiatrist could have a field day unearthing all sorts of traumas and complexes, but I really don't think about it too much." •

"And from that," he put in bitterly, "you went to a grandmother whose idea of saving you was to put the fear of God into you by telling you your mother's sins had tainted you."

She was surprised at his quick grasp of the situation. Again she managed a faint smile. "Sounds like something out of a Steinbeck novel, doesn't it? Anyway," she went on determinedly, before he could unnerve her with more questions and probing looks, "it wasn't all bad. You learn a lot about survival on the streets, you grow up fast, and—you learn to take what you want, because no one is going to give it to you. It didn't take me long to decide that I didn't want that for the rest of my life." Now her voice grew absent, her eyes narrowed thoughtfully on a distant horizon. "I wanted Ward and June Cleaver, the house on Main Street, rose bushes and tupperware...I wanted to make a regular life for myself, you know? So..." She glanced back at him, "I finished school, I studied hard and got good grades. I liked school, especially math. And then I worked at all sorts of jobs to take night courses, and I finally got my degree." She shook her head wonderingly, hardly believing that so much struggle and toil could be so neatly summed up in a few sentences. "It wasn't easy," she added, almost as an afterthought.

"But you made it," he said quietly. There was so much unspoken care and admiration in that simple sentence that the glow which spread over her was like an inner sun.

She nodded, unable to prevent a small, proud tilt of her chin. "I got a job with a New York company, I started fixing up an apartment, and I was on my way." But then she fell silent.

He did not urge her for a while. His eyes upon her were very intent. Then he prompted gently, "What happened, Dusty? How did you end up on that Nevada highway going nowhere?"

She had not thought she would be able to tell him. To her great surprise, now that the moment had come, the words flowed with a curious detachment, strangely emotionless. It hardly seemed to matter any more. "Peter—he was my boss—was kind to me. He was generous, gentle, affectionate—all I ever thought I wanted in a man. He took care of me. He said he loved me, he promised me—oh, everything I thought I had always wanted. I didn't love him," she admitted, the words coming more slowly now as she moved back to examine all the details that had led up to the trauma with peculiar objectivity. "I didn't lie to him about that, but he said it didn't matter, that I would learn to love him. And I wanted so badly to believe him, I wanted to believe that all my dreams could come true—that was when he asked me to fly to Las Vegas to get married, I gave up my apartment and sold all my things, and I really thought it would work. Only..." Her smile was dry, not bitter. "I didn't know Peter as well as I thought I did. He liked to gamble, and he didn't care what he gambled with. My watch, my money...even some of my clothes. And then, when he was down to nothing and couldn't have more money wired in until morning, he dressed me up in that sexy cocktail dress and took me downstairs to meet a couple of men he had been losing to, and told them I would keep them 'entertained' until his money came through. Of course, none of them had in mind a few drinks and stimulating conversation..." Her lips tightened once with that memory, and then, with a breath, she moved on to quickly finish the story. "I slipped away on some excuse—I don't even remember what it was—and threw a few things into an overnight bag. There was fifty dollars stuffed in the back of a drawer—lord knows how he overlooked that—so I took it, thinking I could get a bus ticket to somewhere, anywhere... but I couldn't. So I just started walking." She shook her head slowly. "I wasn't thinking very clearly."

He was silent for a very, very long time. And she simply sat there, waiting for his reaction, feeling clean and purged for having told him, feeling peaceful about herself for the first time since it had begun. Yes, peaceful, and right.

Then Dusty heard his rustle of movement, his arm crooked around the back of her neck very lightly, hardly touching her, his fingers a light, unsteady brush against her cheek. His face moved close, she saw the pain there, the tenderness and the uncertainty in his eyes, his lips touched her temple. Automatically, with a surge of love so great it obscured everything else, she turned her face to his, her hand caressing the warm roughness of his cheek, and just before their lips met she saw within his eyes enough to last her a lifetime. The naked emotion there was filled with tenderness and care, sincerity and depth, it was compassion and adoration and a myriad of other things too complicated and too intense to analyze. His lips fell upon hers, lightly at first, with utmost gentleness and incredible delicacy, caressing her, soothing her, giving of himself and his most fragile emotions with such sweetness that it brought tears to her eyes. Then, as her arms slipped around him and drew him close the communication they shared deepened and intensified, building with need and urgency and powerful, primal emotions that demanded more and more of each other. Only complete sharing would fill the emptiness, becoming a part of one another was the destiny that compelled them, and Dusty knew with a certainty unlike any she had ever experienced before that that was all she wanted. Camp. All of him. To belong to him, to have him belong to her, to merge their lives with their separate pains and individual joys and to make them one....

And then he dragged his lips away from hers, slowly across her face, to rest at last upon her cheek. His breath was warm and unsteady on her skin, she could feel the arms that held her forcefully and slowly begin to relax. "Oh, Dusty..."

he whispered. He kissed her closed eyelids with all the reluctance and tenderness a parent might bestow upon a lost child. The hand that stroked her hair was trembling. "Dusty," he whispered again, and that was all.

She lay within the circle of his arms and the change she could feel growing within him frightened and confused her. Her heart was pounding so hard it threatened to choke her, and slowly, very slowly, he reached up and removed her arms from about his neck. The question in her eyes was met with pain and reluctance in his. "You'd better go to bed now," he said quietly, somewhat hoarsely. "It's late."

Somehow she got to her feet. Confusion was twisting in her head and desperate longing aching in her chest. Then she turned back. Two weeks. If that was all he offered . . .

"Camp," she whispered, and he looked up. "Aren't you—aren't you coming?"

He looked at her for a long time, and each of them knew what lay in the balance with his hesitation. She would accept him on his terms if those were the only terms upon which she could have him, for however brief a time. She wanted him beside her tonight. She loved him and she wanted him for one night or fourteen nights, it did not matter. He looked at her and his eyes were very steady, strangely remote, yet far within their depths lurked a secret sorrow she did not understand. And he said at last, "No." He turned away.

The movement seemed to be excruciating for him. "Not yet."

After another endless moment she turned and walked alone back to the truck.

Chapter Ten

Camp did not come to bed at all that night, or the next two nights. Those two days were the bleakest and most agonizing of Dusty's life. He was remote, indifferent, unfailingly polite—but a stranger to her. Dusty tried not to show how much this was hurting her, but inside a little of her died each time he looked at her with those blank, emotionless eyes, and when he left her alone at night she refused to cry herself to sleep—with the result that she didn't sleep at all.

The worst had happened. Camp knew her now, he knew where she had come from and where she had been, and he was carefully guarding his pedigree from further contamination by alley cat stock. He knew about her mother and it disgusted him. He knew about Peter and he despised her for it. The closeness that had begun between them was completely dissolved by his new defensive shield. Once he had at least wanted her as a bed partner if nothing else, but now she was not even good enough for that. If he still felt any sexual desire for her his better judgment was keeping it carefully under control, and worst of all, as his need seemed to have abruptly diminished, hers had increased tenfold.

Dusty knew she should hate him. Camp had no right to sit in judgment upon her—no one had that right. She should hate him for betraying her trust and despise him for his snobbery. Another Dusty would have confronted him with open castigation and lashing sarcasm, she would never have let him get away with this. But the new Dusty, the one who had discovered love somewhere on the road between Nevada and New Mexico, could not feel anger toward him. She suffered in silence the agony that grew within her with each passing day and tried to force herself to admit that she had misjudged him. She could not even do that. She clung to a small kernel of belief that somewhere inside the remote stranger who now traveled with her was the Camp she loved, the Camp she still needed and wanted with every fiber of her being.

He had planned a route that would take them most of the way across Texas, then through Arkansas, Tennessee, Kentucky, and Ohio before reaching Pennsylvania. Dusty could not help repeatedly pointing out the folly of his choice, telling him that he could hardly have plotted a less efficient course had he tried to reach Pennsylvania by way of Canada. She knew she was nagging and she could feel him forcefully containing his temper. She also suspected that the reason she was prodding him in such a childish way was in an effort to get attention, to provoke some reaction from him even if it was violent. But Camp remained calm, implacable, ignoring her most of the time and treating her with infuriating politeness the remainder of the time. He would not be moved.

The tension that grew between them on the third day was so volatile it practically crackled with static electricity thoughout the cab, and seemed in some way to be only an inner manifestation of the atmosphere that lay over the bleak Texas landscape before them. Dusty hated Texas. The state seemed to go on forever and ever, miles of sand and scrub brush linked together by telephone poles and oil derricks. Every hour on the hour she complained, "Will we ever get out of Texas?" Finally Camp, as close to losing his temper with her as he had come since that long-ago day in the park, snapped, "No!" And then, with his lips grimly compressed and his hands tightening on the wheel, he fixed his eyes straight ahead and did not speak to her again.

A lot of it had to do with the weather. The day was clear but the sun was dull, the sky was not blue and not gray but something in between. The atmosphere was hot, dry, and very still. Even the air seemed heavy and hard to breathe. The oppressive heat and the unearthly stillness made Dusty uneasy, and when Camp called twice on the CB for a weather report she knew his nerves were being affected, too.

It was late afternoon when Dusty, who had taken to studying the map to alleviate boredom, announced, "If you take the next right it will save you forty miles."

He glanced at her disinterestedly, "What's your hurry?"

"That's—" She did some rapid calculation in her head. "Seventy-eight dollars and forty-three cents in fuel savings. Besides," she added, "there's a town that way." She was hungry to see a town. Even if they did not stop, a mere glimpse of civilization was enough to restore her waning spirits.

Perhaps as a method of apologizing for being short with her earlier, Camp took the next right.

They had gone perhaps ten miles down the empty, seldom-traveled road when Dusty sensed something changing. She felt it as clearly as anything she had ever known in her life, and she felt it before she actually looked around to observe the outer manifestations of her strange inner tension. The sky had turned the most peculiar shade of gray-yellow she had ever seen, but it was more than the sky. The very air itself had taken on a grainy yellow-green cast and on either side of them, behind and before them, the desert stood still and relentless, overcast with a misty phosphorescence that made her feel as though they had just passed unknowingly into another dimension. She felt the stillness most acutely. Even through the motion and the noise of the truck she could sense that outside nothing stirred, the birds had gone to their nests, the lizards were hiding under rocks, the snakes were curled up deep underground, and within her the same animal instincts responded to an unknown danger and began to signal swift alarm. Dusty felt the hairs on the back of her neck stir, the atmosphere within the truck was so heavy it was hard to breathe. She said tightly, "Camp—"

Even before looking at him she knew he had sensed it as well. Tension was evident in the lines of his muscles, the set of his lips, and he responded curtly, "I know," and reached for the CB mike.

But it was too late. The first blast of wind shook the glass in the windows and drew an involuntary cry from Dusty. The sky darkened abruptly, and then all light was gone as whirling, lashing sand filled the air, blotting out the windows, flung with wave after wave of howling wind against the truck. Camp swore loudly and worked instinctively to keep the truck on the road while Dusty covered her ears against the pounding of hailstones against metal and tried not to scream. Camp's fear was doubled back and magnified into her own, and she could only see him in waves of gray light that were quickly obscured by new onslaughts of sand and hail. Eventually the windshield wipers clogged and they were plunged into a surrealistic interior mist of yellow darkness, not even the headlights could cut a path into what lay outside.

She was only aware that the truck had stopped

moving when Camp pried her hands away from
her ears. His face seemed pale in this unearthly
light, strained and distorted, and he shouted,
"Are you all right?"

She shook her head violently and wound her
arms around his neck, she felt the steely strength
of his own arms in response and the storm that
raged and roared about them was only another
manifestation of the power that fused them together while they held each other, waiting it out.

Time lost its meaning and it could have been
hours or only minutes that they were captured
and helpless against nature's violence. But the
storm stopped just as abruptly as it had begun,
and after a moment, just as abruptly, Camp released her.

Her muscles ached from straining against him
and her eyes were blurred from having kept them
so long tightly squeezed shut. Outside was a muf-
fled stillness, but within the misty twilight of the
cab tension pounded with a palpable roar, as
though the storm had concentrated its power into
human emotions and left its residual oppression to
smother the occupants inside. It was primal, it was
inexplicable, but it existed between and around
them as surely as did the electricity that practically
snapped between them in the long moment they
looked at each other.

Then Camp muttered an oath and reached
abruptly for the door. "I'm going to check the
damage," he said. His voice was tight and sharp.
"You stay here."

Dusty was shaking. Her nerves were frayed and her temper was at the breaking point. It was as though all the repressed emotions, the hurt, the unspoken need, the boredom, the frustration, and the sense of isolation that Camp had forced upon her — had culminated in the unleashed fury of the storm and she didn't think she could take it any longer.

The longer Camp spent outside, the closer she came to screaming from sheer frustration. He scraped the sand off the windows to let in a dusty filtering of pinkish light and that process seemed to take forever. When he opened the hood she couldn't sit in patient silence any longer and she rolled down the window and demanded harshly, "What are you doing? Let's go!"

"Love to," he shot back, and he closed the hood with a reverberating slam. She could not see his face but his voice was a volcano of seething emotion. "From the looks of it, we're not going to be going anywhere for a while."

It was too much. Ounce by ounce, pressure was being heaped upon her fragile emotional balance and she didn't know how much more she could stand. "You mean we're stranded?" she cried. Everything within her rebelled at the prospect and she felt like screaming aloud in frustration. "We can't be!"

"Thanks for telling me." His voice was ugly with controlled sarcasm. "I could have sworn we were." He strode forward and jerked open the door. His face was drawn with anger and his eyes dark and brittle as he flung himself inside and reached for the CB mike. "And the best part is," he spat at her, "thanks to your 'short-cut' we're stranded in the middle of nowhere on a road that doesn't look like it's been traveled this century— who knows how long it will be before any traffic comes by."

She stared at him until the churning rage and horror within her forced her to jerk her head away. She fought for control. The storm wasn't his fault. It wasn't his fault that they were stuck, but it wasn't hers either. It was just that everything seemed to be mounting up on her and it all came back in some way to Camp's callous behavior and it was all she could do to keep from lashing out at him.

Camp swore viciously when all he received from the CB was static, and he muttered, "Either the storm is interfering with reception or the radio's shot, too. That's just great." He sent her one sharp, impatient glance. "Where the hell are we, anyway?"

Dusty unfolded the crumpled map in her lap and studied it in the frustratingly fading light. "There's a town," she discovered, and her relief over the fact was totally inappropriate, wonderfully exciting—a life-giving oasis in the depths of her despair. "It can't be more than five miles across country—that's not far! We can walk—"

His laugh was bitterly mocking, sharply derisive. "This from the woman who set out to cross the desert in spiked heels and a cocktail dress—

what else could I expect?'' He jerked the map from her. "I think you must have left your brains in that precious purse of yours—let go of the damn map!''

Dusty did not know why that particular image should hurt so. She did not know why his reference to their meeting—that awful night which had cost her so much to explain to him—should twist like a knife in festering flesh, but it did. The understanding with which she had entrusted him, the care with which she had given herself, the tenderness that had bound them together—all of it ruptured in that moment when her breaking point was reached and surpassed. "I'm not going to spend the night stranded in the desert!'' she screamed at him. She jerked at the map and it tore down the middle. "I've been trapped in this truck in the middle of this hell hole state for three days, if I have to spend one more night here I'll go crazy—''

"Nobody's keeping you prisoner, lady!'' he shouted back at her, grabbing the torn piece of map from her hand.

"It's stupid!'' Her voice was tight with rising hysteria. "We can't just sit here and do nothing! It could be days—we could run out of food, water—''

"Shut up!'' Camp shouted at her, and the thunder of his voice struck her like a slap. His face was dark and twisted with unchecked anger, the gleam in his eyes was hard and vicious. "I've had it with your bitching and your whining and your adolescent tantrums, do you hear me? *I've had it!*'' The echo of his rage pinioned her to silence, and in a furious gesture of frustrated impotence, he flung the map to the floor. His face was a mask of controlled violence, his eyes the flame that pushed her over the fine edge of reason. "You may be hell on wheels in a street fight, baby" — he spat contemptuously at her — "give you a chain and a switchblade and you can tear the inner city apart, but out here you're an infant, a helpless fool, a babbling idiot who can't tell the desert from the beach and you will damn well do as I say, is that understood?''

Oh, yes, she understood. All too clearly she understood. Dusty was helpless, completely at the mercy of a man who did not want her, did not care for her, who looked at her now with hatred and contempt in his eyes and suddenly it all snapped within her — the hurt and the anger, the humiliation and rejection, the blinding need that had somehow been perverted into violence, and all she wanted was to get away... away from him, away from this place, away from the pain that was clawing at her like a mad animal....

Her hand was on the door handle, he shouted something at her and she struck at him. The door fell open and the sleeve of her shirt ripped as he grabbed at her, then she was running, blindly and heedless across the unmarked desert with the setting sun kindling a flame in the sky and turning the sand to embers. She slipped on melting hailstones and tripped over sand moguls, and steely hands gripped her shoulders, whirling her around with a force that almost knocked her off her feet; Camp's voice roared like thunder in her ears.

"Don't you ever run away from me again! Camp shook her, and he kept on shaking her as though his greatest pleasure would be to snap her neck. The red haze of twilight whirled and vibrated into a greedy smear before her eyes, but his face was clear, wild with fury, twisted with a killing rage. His eyes were blue flames that seared and tore at her, completely out of control, he shook her and he shouted at her, "You little fool! Don't you ever—"

She struck out at him with a scream of pure primal rage, clawing and kicking, she broke away and the material of her shirt ripped again in his hands. Then a heavy weight knocked her breath away as she hit the sand. She was flung over on her back with her legs pinned between his and his weight on her abdomen while her lungs ached and burned for lost air. His face was a mask of raw emotions, a composite blur of every passion ever experienced to its finest intensity by the human animal—need and rage, lust and greed, desperation, pain, desire, and when her breath returned to straining lungs in a gasp it was immediately stolen from her again by the brutal force of his mouth.

Dusty fought him even though she wanted him. The cry that was swallowed by the driving force of his mouth could have been ecstasy or it could have been rage, as elemental urges too long denied rampaged through them and exploded between them. Mouths that brutalized and devoured, hands that grappled and grasped, passions long since out of control exploded and were refueled with each breath. Above them the dying sun caught refracted particles of sand and ice and blazed the sky with a wash of brilliant scarlet, but between them the flame that roared had the power to ignite the earth. Desperation and despair, violent hunger and fierce need consumed them and ruled them, they fought it and they fought for it and eventually they were carried away by it—both of them helpless against what they had known from the start they could not control.

His hands tore at her clothing and hers ripped at his, she arched to receive him even as her nails dug violent streaks down the course of his back. Stronger than passion, deeper than nature, it was the essence of all that had ever been loved and lost, the quintessence of what has been desperately sought and found at last, it was beyond the depth of human emotion and it shook the soul. They were the violence of the storm, the brilliance of the flaming desert, the crystal of refracted joy and the effervesence of a shooting star, they were a part of all that is basic to the universe; they were one. In one shuddering explosion of fire and passion the earth and sky around them blazed and stretched and exploded again with blinding power, and the shimmering, searing glow seemed to last forever. Red-misted light drifted down upon them like the embers of a burning universe, and at last they were still.

It was dark when some form of muted consciousness finally began to stir within Dusty. Stars had magically appeared in a midnight blue sky and they were so large and so brilliant they reminded her of prisms on a crystal chandelier. Camp lay beside her, his warmth permeating every pore of her skin and deflecting the chill air that surrounded them, though he did not touch her. His breathing was ragged, Dusty hardly breathed at all.

She felt stripped, purged, cleansed and purified, born again and waiting for his touch to give her life. Her mind was battered and numb; conscious thought was an alien process. What they had just shared defied understanding or definition; it was beyond either of them yet it was a part of both of them, it had changed forever what they were or ever hoped to be.

She loved him. Among the muted vortex of battered emotions that one thing was clear, and even that was not a conscious thought. She belonged to him. They had met in violence and been forged in the fires of passion into a union no power could break. Each of them had fought in their own way and for their own reasons what they knew must inevitably become of them, they had lost the battle and gained...what? Even Dusty could not answer that. In the act of domination—if that was what it was—he had captured the last stronghold of her heart; whether he wanted it or not it was his. She had surrendered herself to him completely and for all time, and whatever hope she had nourished toward preserving her independence was gone. She simply belonged to him, she was dependent upon him for more than simple survival now—he held her very life in the palm of his hand. And what would become of her now? What was he thinking, what was he feeling?

He stood abruptly and began to pull on his jeans. "Get dressed," he commanded. His voice was harsh. "It's cold out here."

And then she knew. She knew with a wave of agony so intense it numbed her from the inside out. He did not love her. He had never claimed to love her. He had wanted her as one animal wants another and he had taken her in the same way. Now that it was over he was disgusted with himself and he despised her for dragging him down to her depths. Her heart belonged to him and he did not want it. He did not even see it.

She dressed with numb fingers that were surprisingly steady, and tears were frozen in her throat. She did not think she would ever cry again. Some pains were too deep for tears, some losses too intense for grief.

His grip upon her arm was steely and impersonal as they walked back to the truck. When they reached it he said tonelessly, "It's too dark to do anything about the truck tonight. I'll start work on it at first light. Meanwhile, we may as well get some rest."

She stared at him, and some part of her mind was wondering apathetically why he was talking about the truck, about resting, about the things normal people did and thought in the normal world when everything about her life had just been ripped from its roots and tossed to the wind... And in his eyes, after a moment, she thought she saw something of the same dull reflection, a sort of numb shock as though he had only just realized what he had said and couldn't believe it was his voice that had spoken. Then, as she watched beneath the cold filtering starlight, those eyes slowly filled with pain, the harsh blank planes of his face softened and then tightened as though with the effort to subdue inner agony. She watched the transformation in detachment and mild wonder, and he whispered hoarsely, "Dusty, I'm sorry. I—"

He was apologizing. He was sorry. She couldn't accept that, she couldn't take it on top of everything else and if she heard another word everything within her would shatter into a million irretrievable fragments... She spoke quickly, automatically, in a voice that was calm and amazingly cool. "Don't be," she said. Her gaze met his evenly and emptily. "I like it better this way. All paid up. You got what you wanted and I've got a ticket east, it's a fair trade."

She saw the swift flare of redoubled hurt and disbelief in his eyes, she heard his sharp intake of breath, but she turned away before it could affect her. She opened the door and gripped the handrail to pull herself inside. "I'll sleep in front," she volunteered dully.

For just another moment, there was nothing, absolutely nothing behind her. Then his hand was hard on her arm and his voice was like iron. "No," he said grimly. "You sleep with me, where I know where you are. You're not going to run away again."

She did not look at him, she did not protest. She did not know that emotional and physical shock were taking their toll on both her body and her mind, she only knew that suddenly the energy for thought and reason and even for movement were fast becoming beyond her means. She stumbled getting into the back and the look Camp gave her as he caught her was sharp with concern, raw with things unspoken—things she refused to hear, refused even to see.

She lay beside him on the mattress where they had lain together so many times before and the basic protective instinct that hinged Dusty's fragile emotions together refused to acknowledge that this night was any different. She lay beside him not touching him, hardly aware of him, wrapped in the blessed anesthesia of shock, and she closed her eyes.

Sometime during the night she awoke. Camp's arm was around her, his bare shoulder was wet with her silent tears. What she refused to allow sleep released, and even as she opened her eyes tears continued to flow, numbly, helplessly, unthinkingly. He lay still and wakeful beneath the burden of his own silent misery, and he held her throughout the night.

Chapter Eleven

Dusty awoke alone the next morning. It was stifling hot inside the truck without the air-conditioning and she could hear Camp working beneath the hood. She turned over bleakly and stared into the smothering folds of the vinyl-shrouded twilight and tried to find the courage to face another day.

There was no residual shock to shield her from the stark reality this morning. She had to face it, to look back over it with as much calmness as she could and somehow learn to live with it—for ten more days, for the rest of her life. The memory should have been shameful, but it was not. What had happened between them was out of their control; it was as though the violence of the storm had triggered the violence of repressed emotions within them and they had been helpless victims of an instinct as old as man. Two people scared and alone fighting desire until control snapped and physical release was the most basic way to deal with emotions too complicated to handle...the only difference was, one of those people had been in love. The other had only been desperate.

She could not hate him, or herself. She wished she could stop loving him but she couldn't. She wished she could stop needing him, but she could not even do that. It was done, it was history, it could not be taken back. Dusty had to face it, and somehow, she had to go on knowing that nothing had changed about her feelings for him, they had only intensified. And knowing that if anything had changed in his feelings for her, it was not for the better.

Dusty was strong. She had always been strong, and she knew she could handle this. She loved him, and loving him gave her a courage she had never known before.

She dressed and hid her soiled and torn clothing in a corner, then she went outside, ready to face whatever was in his eyes. She was not even surprised to find that there was nothing in Camp's eyes, that in fact, he avoided looking at her whenever possible and if his gaze happened to skim toward her when he thought she wasn't looking it was covered again before anything was revealed. They were once again stiff and polite with each other, carefully neutral, each of them cautiously avoiding making the first move.

Camp explained to her what engine damage had been done but she did not try to understand it. He told her he thought he could effect a patch job until they could make further repairs, and that was all she was interested in. The desert sun was broiling at midmorning and no one came by on the flat Texas road. Dusty tried to contact someone on the emergency CB channel but all she got was static. She suspected the antenna had been damaged during the storm.

She brought him cups of water from the ice that was melting in the coolers, which he accepted gratefully, pausing only long enough to drink it before returning to work again. The heat was merciless. His T-shirt would be dripping with perspiration one minute and stiff and dry the next, even his hat was dark around the band and skull. As Dusty stood beside him she could feel the sun sap away her energy in great radiant waves until she had to repeatedly keep blinking her eyes to dispel the spots of dizziness. It was no cooler in the truck, and besides, she couldn't make herself leave him to work in that inferno by himself— even if she could not help, simply being with him was enough.

He looked at her suddenly, and the sharp tone of his voice startled her. "What do you think you're doing out here?" he demanded. His face, rouged with exertion and glossy with perspiration, was tight. She mistook the alarm in his eyes for anger. "Why aren't you in the truck where you belong?"

"I'm not hurting anything," she defended. She found it utterly impossible to gather the energy to return his anger. "I'm staying out of your way— I'm just watching."

His face was grim and his eyes dark as he

gripped her arm and pulled her toward the truck. "You're as white as a sheet. Do you want to end up with a case of heat exhaustion on top of everything else? Don't you know this sun can be fatal?"

"You were outside," she protested weakly as she climbed inside the truck.

Camp's hands on her waist steadied her. "I'm used to it," he retorted, and when her knees buckled at the front seat he caught her and helped her into the back.

Dusty collapsed on the mattress, breathing hard, suddenly dizzy. It was hot and airless inside and her skin felt as though it was on fire. He was angry with her again and it wasn't her fault—how much longer could she endure his anger when all she wanted was his love?

She started to sit up but he pushed her down again, and his hands deftly undid the zipper of her jeans and began to tug the garment from her hips. She couldn't help gasping, instinctively she pushed his hands away and the look in his eyes froze her.

"Don't worry," he said shortly. Bitterness and self-loathing churned in his eyes and tore at her heart before he looked away. His lips were tight and grim. "I won't attack you." He pulled the jeans over her ankles and flung them away, and she fell back weakly, staring at him.

His back was to her as he turned to soak a towel in ice water from the cooler, the taut shoulders and the bleak profile exhibited such misery, such inner anger, that she wanted to reach out and comfort him, to soothe away his pain. But he had shielded himself from her, she was afraid to touch him. "Camp..." she ventured tremulously.

He turned. In controlled, efficient movements he lifted her head and placed the cold towel against the back of her neck, with another he began to sponge her face and her wrists and the backs of her knees. His touch was impersonal, his face a blank, and she watched him, aching with agony for him, desperately yearning to reach him.

And then his eyes met hers and the swift explosion of pain within his face completely caught her off guard. "Will you stop looking at me like that?" he cried. "Don't you think I know—don't you think I feel rotten enough as it is?"

He turned abruptly away, one fist pressed against his tightly compressed lips, the other closing about the damp towel until streams of water ran over his white knuckles. She struggled to sit up, fighting a throbbing wave of dizziness, and this time she could not stop herself, she reached out to lightly touch his shoulder.

He flinched from her touch and she dropped her hand. His breath was long and harsh, his voice tight and heavy with self-hatred. "From the beginning," he said lowly, "I knew your needs were special. I saw you had been hurt, I knew how used you were to being used and I saw what it had done to you. I made up my mind I was not going to be another of the users." It was as though some inner demon compelled him to speak out loud, to seek understanding if not expiation, and the process was excruciating for him.

Dusty felt everything within her begin to soften in response to him, loving him was like a mountain pool that was fed from the stream of his words, renewed and refreshed with each word, each gesture, each breath he took. "As much as I wanted you," he continued deliberately, with an effort, "it was not going to be at the expense of your self-esteem...you had so much to offer besides your body and I wanted all that you could give me, I wanted to add to your life, not take away from it." The last was cut off with a harsh breath and a tightening of his shoulders and she felt tears of love and gratitude prick her eyelids. Her hand fluttered again to touch him, but fell when the stiffening of his muscles sensed the movement and he went on. "Later—after I knew what you had really suffered, how hard you had fought against such incredible odds to become the very special and very precious person you are... When I knew you, and realized how desperately you were holding on to your dreams by fragile threads—I saw myself for the selfish bastard I was. And no matter how I looked at it or tried to justify it, what I was really doing was using you and it was something you couldn't afford. How could I take you for a two-week love affair knowing that you needed so much more? How could I leave you at the end of that time with nothing more than 'thanks for a good time' when I knew what that would do to you? I swore to myself I would never hurt you like that." And his voice fell to hardly more than a rough whisper, "I swore I would never hurt you."

Camp turned suddenly and his face was torn with self-hatred, his eyes narrowed and blazing. "So what did I do? I used you in the most violent and debasing way a man can use a woman, I hurt you in a way you'll never forget... and I can't forgive myself for that, Dusty." His eyes closed slowly, the breath he drew through barely parted lips was long and unsteady. "I certainly don't expect you to."

She looked at him, knowing that he suffered because of her even as she suffered with him and her throat was so tight and full that she couldn't speak. This was all she loved about him, the honor, the openness, the caring, the sincerity... yet, the very things she loved were tearing him apart and how could she ease his pain?

When he looked at her again his eyes were fierce and determined, the set of his mouth grim. He said simply, "It won't happen again. If you don't believe anything else I've said—and Lord knows why you should—believe that. I'll get you out of here, I'll take you back East where things are green and you can start over... and you'll never have to see me again. I promise you that."

She could not stay silent any longer. She shook her head violently, her eyes flooded and glistened with tears, and she choked, "No!" She touched his arm and he did not draw away. She could not help it, the love and the yearning she felt for him were etched into desperate lines on her face, she had to tell him, to make him see that all she ever wanted was to be with him... "Camp, don't do this to yourself—to me! Don't you see that last night—doesn't matter..." Oh, it did matter. It mattered more than anything else in her life, but not the way he imagined. "I love you, Camp," she whispered, trying to keep her voice from breaking. "Please see that. I loved you before and—last night doesn't make any difference. We both said some cruel and—impulsive things, but I didn't mean... I didn't feel used." The whisper was barely audible, and she dropped her eyes, suddenly remembering the cold reference she had made to her "payment" and ashamed of it. "I love you," she finished simply, on a breath. "I only want to be with you. That's all."

His hand lightly touched her hair. When she lifted her eyes to him she saw tenderness, sorrow, and even perhaps a small flicker of wonder twisted into the pain that darkened his blue eyes. His fingers moved against a strand of her hair as though she were a fragile vessel he was afraid of breaking, and then he dropped his hand. The expression that came over his face then crept in by degrees until it was carefully blank, his tone neutral. "Don't love me, Dusty," he said tiredly. "I have nothing for you. I'm a maverick, a criminal, a runaway. I'll steal your dreams and give you nothing in return. Pennsylvania is the end of the line for us, you know that. You'll have a chance there, and I'll..." A slow bleakness crossed his face and his eyes wandered away from her, toward the window and out to the desert. "... be moving on," he said simply, finally.

But it wasn't that easy for her. He had nothing for her, he could not return her love, but how could she simply stop loving him? What meaning would a new life in the verdant east have for her when every landscape would be a desert without him?

She turned away from him, her eyes closed and her lips tightly compressed to still the trembling. It suddenly seemed that all of her life had been leading up to this moment, the time when she would find her heart and give it and receive nothing in return...the time when past goals were only shadows of present emptiness and she discovered that the only thing she really wanted was the one thing she couldn't have. There was no place for her in his life. He didn't want her.

She felt his lips brush her temple lightly just before he got up. "I'm sorry," he whispered hoarsely. He sat there a moment looking at her, his hand cupped in the air just above her hair as though he were fighting the urge to touch her, and she could not face the battle that tore at his face. She did not want to see the pity his eyes held. He got up abruptly and left her, and she turned her head weakly to the pillow and could not even cry.

They made it to the nearest town by mid-afternoon. Camp was able to get the parts there to make permanent repairs on the truck, and they spent one more night in Texas. The next morning he abruptly took a northward course that put the Great State behind them by midday. He continued steadily on a direct northern course that did not meander around back roads or waste time with circuitous routes, and Dusty knew that Camp was impatient to reach their destination—and be rid of her.

Yet nothing in his attitude revealed his urgency to part her company. If anything, he was kinder to her, more talkative, more entertaining. She tried to respond to his need to make their last days together pleasant, for in truth she wanted it even more than he did, but it was an effort for her and she suspected he saw that.

Dusty's brush with heat exhaustion had left her drained and weak, and though she tried to hide it from him, her pallor and lethargy worried Camp. He went out of his way to point out things of interest along the road, trying to pick up her spirits and make her laugh, and always when he succeeded the lightening of the lines on his face, which had grown increasingly prominent the last few days, was well worth the effort it cost her. He stopped often to rest, tempting her with gastronomic treats from every town through which they passed, offering to take her on sight-seeing tours but not objecting when she refused. He was gentle, considerate, instinctively caring, and every day Dusty only loved him more.

But he did not want her to love him. That she

knew. More than once, Dusty caught him looking at her with such sorrow and longing in his eyes that she knew immediately his pain was prompted by guilt, and guilt was one thing she refused to allow him. She always met such looks with a quick bright smile, and always he turned away with a frown of concern creasing his brow. Sometimes he looked as though he would say something, but she never gave him a chance. She did not want explanations or apologies from him, for he owed her neither. She had not expected love from him, and she was sorry that hers for him had only added to his burden. He was right, she could see that now—there was nothing for them together. He cared for her, that she could not deny, but Camp cared for her in the same way he cared for all life's castaways—the strays, waifs, and derelicts no one else wanted. He had felt desire for her, he felt pity for her, but she did not belong in his life. He belonged with some gentle, refined and soft-spoken Boston girl, the perfect wife and hostess, the mother to three or four of his beautiful, perfectly mannered children... He had no use for a renegade streetfighter like Dusty. Simply by taking her in and letting her love him, he had given her more than she had any right to ask for or expect, she would not ask him for anything else.

Dusty treasured their days together and did her best to make them bright and easy for him, even though the effort left her drained and weary in body and spirit. At night they lay down together and did not touch but sometimes Dusty would awake with her head pillowed on his chest and his arms around her, knowing that he was awake too. Neither of them ever acknowledged it in the morning, and Camp continued his efforts to make the travel light and easy while Dusty quietly buried a heart that refused to break.

It wasn't until they reached the rolling hills of Kentucky that Dusty felt the first stirrings of real life within her again. All around them lush greenery flourished in every imaginable shade, from pale lime to rich emerald. Summer roses and marigolds and snapdragons and zinnia burst with color in unexpected places, and for Dusty—starved as she was for the sight of living things—every bed of color was like a bonus to the wealth of green that filled her eyes and her nostrils and even seemed to exude a soft sensory music only her ears could hear. Her face became animated as she turned this way and that, and Camp noticed with relief and approval as color began to return to her cheeks and a sparkle grew in her eyes. After a time of excitedly pointing out one spot of beauty and then another she turned to him, a small puzzled frown troubling her brow and she inquired, "Where's the blue grass?"

His eyes twinkled. "In the imagination of some Kentucky poet, I don't doubt. I hope you won't be too disappointed; I'm afraid all the grass in Kentucky is the same boring green."

She shook her head, her cheeks dimpling with pleasure as she turned again to look out the window. "Blue is a stupid color for grass anyway. Oh, look!" She pointed to a portrait-perfect view of glossy roan thoroughbreds standing beside a white fence, and Camp relaxed against the seat, feeling tension that was so deeply ingrained he had not even been aware of it draining away from him with every word, every child-like gesture, every laugh of pleasure she made.

It was mid-afternoon when they reached Lexington; Dusty was surprised when he pulled into a large, modern motel parking lot and stopped. At her questioning look he explained, "I thought we both could use a good night's rest in a real bed, a bath in a real bathtub and maybe a meal in a restaurant that rates more than one star. What do you say?"

It would have been difficult for anything to destroy her mood, even though she knew when he said "real bed" what he really meant was separate beds. Separate rooms. But a bath sounded nice, so did a clean, inviting motel room, and she felt the stirrings of her appetite for the first time in days. She nodded enthusiastically and her mood was celebratory as they went inside.

Her room was perfect. Large and airy with rolling hills and thoroughbreds etched on the light wallpaper, it contained all the commodities of the real world she had almost forgotten existed... carpeting, a dresser, upholstered chairs, and tasteful beige lamps, mirrors and a fully equipped bathroom. She almost laughed out loud in delight.

She turned to Camp and his eyes sparkled at her evident pleasure. "It will do," she pronounced haughtily, and he winked at her.

"It had better," he retorted. He set her toilet articles on the dresser and turned toward the door. "I have some things to do around town this afternoon; I'll check back with you in a couple of hours." The door was open when he turned back, a very strange look on his face. "Dusty..." he insisted quietly, his eyes uncertain, "You will be here, won't you?"

She looked at him and her answer was evident in her eyes. It was impossible for her to leave him, or even try, ever again. "Yes," she answered softly. "I'll be here."

He looked at her for a moment longer, and then left abruptly.

Dusty did not know what to do first—turn on the color television set or fill the tub with steamy water or simply walk around barefoot on the carpet. It was amazing how drastically one could miss the conveniences of civilization that were usually taken for granted, how quickly one came to depend upon them and how greatly one could hunger for them without even realizing it when they were gone. In the end she stretched out carefully on the full-sized, gold-colored bedspread, refusing to think about the empty pillow and the night she would spend alone, and she fell within minutes into the first completely peaceful sleep she had had in weeks.

She awoke two hours later refreshed, relaxed and feeling good. She could tell by the view from the window that sunset was near, and she wondered where Camp was. Perhaps he, too, had decided to have a nap. He could use it, she knew.

With renewed energy and spurred enthusiasm for the dinner he had promised, she got up and filled the tub with steamy clear water, wishing for a capful of bubbles but anticipating the bath with such relish that it hardly mattered. She washed her hair and rinsed out her underwear to dry over the sink while she soaked, then gave herself over to the full sensual pleasure of the brimming tub.

She luxuriated until the water grew cool, purging her mind as well as her body of all the dread and the worry and unpleasantness that had clung to her the past week and beyond. This was Kentucky, their time together was drawing to a close. But tonight, tomorrow—for as long as they had— was theirs. The memories made now would be the treasures she stored for the rest of her life and she would not taint it with the sorrow that must be faced soon enough.

She dried herself and pulled on Camp's long-sleeved shirt while she returned to the bedroom for her hairbrush. On the threshold she stopped, her hand fluttering to her lips with a gasp of pure pleasure, her eyes widening with wonder and delight.

Upon the bed was one of the prettiest dresses she had ever seen. It was a pale blue voile sundress overprinted with a watercolor landscape design in whispering hues of pastels—lavender, yellow and green. The bodice was low and square with spaghetti straps, the skirt full from a tapered waist and trimmed with a deep ruffle. There was a matching ruffled shawl and a delicate pair of small-heeled white sandals and even a white leather clutch purse.

"Do you like it?" Camp inquired behind her. There was a trace of anxiety in his tone which vanished immediately when he saw her face.

"Like it? Oh, Camp, it's beautiful—it's like Christmas!" Her first instinct was to fling her arms around him in gratitude and the only thing that stopped her was the sight of him standing before her like she had never seen him before.

He was wearing a light colored suit and a very pale rose shirt open at the collar. Freshly shaven and groomed, his hair was a gleaming panoply of bronze and gold, his deep tawny tan making his eyes look like crystal blue mirrors. She had never imagined Camp in a suit before, and he wore it as though he were born to it—as of course he would. The effect was magnificent; it took her breath away.

He smiled when he saw she was staring at him, and she turned away quickly, fingering the lovely garment and stammering, "H-how did you know my size?"

"Easy." His smile deepened as he came over to her. "I just told the lady I wanted the size to fit a woman with the perfect figure—the size every woman wishes she was and very few are."

Dusty blushed. She had not expected him to say that. She held the dress up to her, her eyes and her cheeks glowing as she pressed it to her body, and she declared, "Well, however you did it, it looks like a perfect fit—oh!"

That exclamation of renewed delight was caused by the discovery that he had even remembered stockings, a pale blue half slip and...a pair of French-cut bikini panties of the same hue trimmed with ivory lace. "Oh," she said again, and when she glanced at him his smile was rueful, though his eyes twinkled.

"Those I couldn't resist," he half-apologized, though in his eyes was no sign of apology at all. The thought of his choosing intimate apparel for her made her face tingle and her heart speed with a strange mixture of embarrassment and anticipation, and the way he looked at her just then caused her stomach to clench in instinctive anticipation. His eyes traveled over her as though on a compulsion, noticing the way the thin material of his shirt hugged her curves and clung to the damp patches of her skin. Then he jerked his eyes away and suggested somewhat huskily, "Why don't you get dressed? I'll wait for you here."

And as she quickly gathered up her new clothes and turned toward the bathroom he added with mock severity. "And don't take all night—I'm starved!"

It was, indeed, a night that would live forever. They went to a restaurant within walking distance, where the cuisine was superb and the atmosphere casually elegant. There was a dance floor and the band played soothingly danceable ballads to the background clink of silver and crystal and the murmur of soft conversation.

Dusty was completely enchanted. There were sprays of ferns surrounding a single white candle on each linen-covered table and the waiters were liveried in red and black. Dusty could not decide whether she wanted to look first at a menu or dance, but with competent mastery Camp made that decision for her. He ordered the wine with a knowledgeable ease that reminded her of his background, and then he led her to the dance floor.

Camp was, of course, a superb dancer. His movements were fluid and graceful and in his arms she melted into his natural rhythm that was impossible not to follow. When he smiled down at her he did not have to tell her she was beautiful; she felt beautiful, she felt perfect, she was all she had ever wanted to be and she had all she had ever hoped for. She knew suddenly and without a doubt that, though it may last no more than one night, the one night was worth it all.

When they were seated again he looked at her contentedly across the candlelit table and at last pronounced softly, "Good. I was right."

Her eyes widened questioningly. "About what?"

"The dress. It matches your eyes perfectly. I couldn't be sure," he explained, "because your eyes are so many shades of blue—sometimes azure, sometimes cornflower, sometimes close to violet. But I like them best the way they are now in the candlelight—cloud blue, the color of the dress." And his eyes wandered lower, over her pleasure-flushed face, to her naturally rouged lips and her slim neck . . . to the soft white expanse of shoulders and chest which had been saved from burning in the desert sun by his shirts, and then to the thrust of her bosom as it was embraced by the light blue-patterned material. The smile that hovered over his lips and softened his face was a caress that stroked her heart, and the sincerity of his compliment had reached her very soul. "You look"—he said simply—"the way you should always look."

"Happy," she said softly, and he lifted his wine glass to her.

"To Dusty," he said quietly. "May the beauty of your spirit—whether in desert or forest—flourish forever."

She lowered her eyes with a rush of warm pleasure that tingled her skin and throbbed with sudden glowing ecstasy in her chest. *I love you, Camp.* She thought it so intensely, so deeply, that he must surely have sensed it as though the words were spoken out loud. *I love you.*

Dusty had never tasted filet mignon before, and Camp delighted in her enjoyment of her first encounter with the succulent bacon-wrapped beef as though it had been his own. Everything about the meal was exquisite, from the garden-fresh salad to the country-rich butter and freshly baked bread, to the heady red wine that had the deceptively sweet taste of fruit nectar and the crisp bite of a potent intoxicant. When he magnanimously invited her to choose anything she liked from the dessert menu she gave him a mischievous go-for-broke look and extravagantly ordered cherries jubilee, because she had never had a flaming dessert before, and this was the night for firsts.

He laughed with indulgent delight at her childlike enthusiasm. "I've lived with you for two weeks," he accused, his eyes twinkling, "and I never knew it."

"Knew what?" she demanded, finishing off her wine.

"That you're a closet glutton with champagne tastes," he returned.

"Speaking of champagne—"

"Oh, no." He lifted his hand in mock sternness. "No champagne. You've been drinking that wine as though it were colored water and it is very poor taste to have your date carry you out bodily from a place like this."

Her date. The phrase sent a new glow of warmth and wonder through her. Being with Camp in the environment in which he belonged, sharing with him this part of his life Dusty had never been able to fully imagine before, was an experience in closeness and discovery that brought a whole new dimension to loving him. Whether dressed in faded jeans and a battered cowboy hat behind the wheel of an eighteen-wheeler or wearing a stylishly casual suit and ordering wines whose names she could not even pronounce, this was Camp, the man she loved, and she said impulsively, "Oh, Camp, don't you ever miss it all?"

His smile was mildly puzzled. "What?"

"This." She made a small gesture with her

wrist to include the restaurant, the meal, even his clothes. "The quiet life, the real world...don't you ever..." she ventured, and it was genuine curiosity and concern that prompted the question, "want to just settle down?"

He dropped his eyes; the smile faded. Long brown fingers absently caressed the stem of his glass and he answered quietly, after a moment, "Yes. I miss it. Sometimes I hate the road as much as you do, Dusty, sometimes I want nothing more than to just settle down and have a normal life, but..." He let the sentence go unfinished.

She could not drop it that easily. "Why is it so hard for you to go back?" she insisted gently.

He sighed, his eyes wandered around the room absently. "I don't know," he answered at last. "At first it was pride—the same reluctance to admit I was wrong, that got me into this mess in the first place. Because I was wrong," he told her, his eyes steady upon hers. "I know it now and I knew it then but—it's always been hard for me to face my mistakes, and do something about them. I suppose it has something to do with the fact that my father always taught me 'Campbells don't make mistakes.'" His eyes left hers, he sipped his wine. "Anyway, the further I ran the harder it became to turn back, until now..." Again he trailed off.

After a moment she inquired hesitantly, "Are you afraid—of the charges against you? Do you think you might have to go to jail?"

"I don't know," he answered her last question.

"It's possible, I suppose. But it's not a matter of fear as much as it is shame." He dropped his eyes again, growing increasingly uncomfortable; Dusty could sense the lovely mood of the evening disperse like shimmering bubbles in the air. "It's very complicated," he said heavily, and then he looked at her and the expression in his eyes was strangely intense, troubled and anxious as he struggled to make her understand something that she knew instinctively was perhaps the most important thing she would ever hear. "Dusty, I want you to understand that I—"

But the dessert arrived then, and Dusty was not certain whether to be relieved or disappointed. The somber, worried look in his eyes faded as he turned his attention to the waiter and Dusty made an elaborate show of enthusiasm, but her enjoyment of the extravaganza was somewhat diminished. She could not help wondering what he had been about to say that had seemed so very important to him...and she was not certain she had really wanted to hear it.

They walked back to the motel beneath a balmy neon-lit night with their arms around each other's waists. Dusty's head rested against his shoulder and the hypnotic effect of the wine, the evening, the rich green earth that seemed to breathe its life-giving oxygen directly into her lungs, made it all seem perfectly right, and natural—as though it should be that way forever.

In her room Camp pressed her key into her hand and smiled indulgently. "I think I know someone who's going to be slightly hung over in the morning." He bent to brush her forehead with a kiss. "Better get some rest."

But she could not let him go that casually. What he had given her tonight was a culmination of all he had given her, all that filled her heart to overflowing with love and gratitude. Perhaps it was the wine that released inhibitions, for she had no thought of rejection as she looped her arms around his neck and looked up at him, glowing. "Thank you, Camp," she said softly, with all the sincerity of her soul, "for the most wonderful evening of my life."

His hands came up to cup her face, his palms against her cheeks and his thumbs brushing a gentle, repetitive circular motion over her temples. His smile lay deep within his eyes. "There have been a lot of evenings in your life," he reminded her. "Was this really the best?"

Her answer was in her eyes, in the huskiness of her emotion-charged whisper, in the firmness of her nod. "Yes."

The light in his eyes deepened, slowly charging with an emotion that was deeper than contentment as his eyes traveled over her radiant face, memorizing and adoring every inch of it, resting at last on her lips as he said softly, "I wanted it to be." And he kissed her.

The shawl fluttered to the floor as she lifted herself into his embrace, receiving and giving a kiss that was achingly tender and electrifyingly passionate, the kiss that came from the heart and drew at the soul. Pressing each other closer and closer with the desperate need to share and to give and to belong, the kiss was a physical symbol of emotions too deep for expression, emotions that spurred and ignited physical awareness in a way they had never allowed themselves to experience before. His fingers explored with delicacy and contained need, the dip of her waist and the curve of her buttocks, the ridges of her spine as though each one was a wonder of powerful magnitude, his thighs strained against hers and his chest was the pressure of an erratic heartbeat against her breasts. "Oh Dusty," he whispered, "let me make love to you...slowly, wonderfully...as I've always wanted to..."

Her whole mind, her body, and her soul echoed the whisper, "Yes..."

Dusty discovered in his arms that night even more of him to love, the last of him, all of him. She had known the passion, now she knew the tenderness. Each were part of the same man, inextricable and inseparable, components of all that she loved. With slow wonder he undressed her, delighting in each discovery and prolonging each exploration to its fullest extent. She learned to know him with her hands and her eyes and her lips as he kept no part of himself secret from her, accepting pleasure with the same intense wonder as he gave it. In mutual joy and discovery they shared the most profound depths of human need, and their union at last was so sweet, so intense, that it brought tears of sheer happiness to Dusty's eyes. Wrapped around each other and locked within the heart of each other they strove to maintain this state of perfect oneness forever; present reality slipped away and blended into a place where nothing existed except the two of them and what they became together, a shimmering ecstasy rich with the knowledge that they would never be separate again.

Wrapped within the tangle of his arms and legs, her head upon his shoulder and his lips against her hair, the peaceful contentment that sheltered Dusty was the truth that she had found in the arms of this man—all she had ever wanted, all she ever strove for, and more. The battle was over, the search was ended, she had found her life by giving it to the man she loved.

His lips brushed her temple, his soft smile filtered down to her through the darkness. "Are you happy?" he whispered.

So happy that she could not answer. She could only nod against his chest, her hand spreading over his breast, caressing him, loving him.

His arms tightened about her once, and then he relaxed against the pillows, holding her. "Good." His voice was husky, peacefully drowsy. "I always want it to be this way . . . I only want to make you happy."

Later she would wonder whether he had said "want" or "wanted" . . . whether those precious murmured words had really implied a promise of the future, or only a debt paid from the past. But at that moment it didn't matter. At that moment she was in the arms of the man she loved and she would never want for anything again.

Two days later they were in Philadelphia—well ahead of schedule. Those had been two nights of ecstasy that only intensified with every union, two nights of wordless sharing and knowing, two nights of unspoken promises and happiness so blinding that Dusty forgot all the reasons she had dreaded their arrival in Philadelphia.

Once again Camp booked a motel room. He still had several days before his next load and she looked forward to spending the time with him in the leisure of comfortable surroundings—a kitchenette, a living suite, all the comforts of home. Once again Camp had errands to run in the afternoon, and when he returned he seemed restless and ill-at-ease. Over dinner he was mostly silent, and his lovemaking that night was intensely passionate, almost desperate. It was his mood that reminded Dusty that so much was still unsettled between them, so much had been left unspoken . . . things that she, perhaps, had been subconsciously trying to avoid because she treasured so desperately what had grown between them these past few days, and was afraid to threaten it with reality.

But as she lay in his arms that night, sensing his tension and his anxiety, she could not avoid it any longer. "Camp," she said softly, tilting her head on his chest to look at his face in the dimness. "I don't want to stay here, you know. I want to go with you—to stay with you on the road. I can keep your books or—"

· His soft intake of breath told her that that was what he had been waiting to hear. For a moment the fingers that had been caressing her shoulder tightened, then forcefully relaxed. He said, in a voice that sounded cautiously teasing, "Come on, honey, you know you'd hate that. You get motion sickness. My music gets on your nerves. The desert makes you crazy. You'd be ready for the men in little white jackets inside a month."

Cautiously, she let her own body relax, her head resting against his chest again. "I don't know," she murmured, "it kind of grows on you. I guess I've gotten used to it. I would probably go through some kind of withdrawal if I had to wake up without the smell of diesel in the air for too many mornings." Besides, there was no choice. He could not stay here and she could not stay without him, and there simply was no choice.

He smiled a little, and when he spoke again there was an odd tone to his voice, serious, reserved, warily probing. "What about your house in the suburbs? Your nine-to-five routine? I thought that was what you wanted."

That was what she wanted . . . once. Before she discovered there was something she wanted more, something she could not live without... She shook her head against his chest. "It doesn't matter," she whispered.

Camp was silent for so long that her heart began to pound with unspoken anxiety. Did he not want her with him? Had nothing changed for him in the past few days? He had never said he loved her. He wanted her, but did that desire extend to making her a part of his independent, free-spirited life? Anxiety stirred and coiled within her, and she lifted her face to him once again. "Camp..."

His arms tightened about her reassuringly. "Let's not talk about it tonight," he soothed. "Get some sleep."

She lay against his chest again, but she could not sleep. "I can't help it, Camp," she whispered at last. Her voice sounded uneven and broken in the dark. "I love you."

He moved to place one soft, exquisitely tender kiss upon her temple. "I know," he whispered. That was all he said. "I know." Why did those two simple words make her feel so insanely secure?

When Dusty awoke she was alone.

She knew she should have been prepared for it. In that frozen moment of awful truth when she reached for Camp and he was not there, some part of her mind was telling her calmly that she had always known this day would come. There was no reason for the paralyzing shock, the cold horror, the smothering sensation of betrayal that was pounding down on her. He had never made her any promises. From the beginning it had been agreed that Philadelphia would mark the parting of their ways.... He had never made any promises.

She struggled to sit up beneath a weight that was like swimming toward the surface of a cold mountain pool—frantic for air and despairing of ever reaching the top. Why was it so hard to believe? How had she let herself imagine that all she felt for him was returned? Nothing had changed for him with the few ecstatic nights they had shared in each other's arms... He had freely admitted to wanting her. He had always been honest with her about that. He never made mention of anything more. Never...

Yet still, desperate, disbelieving eyes searched around the room, her broken voice choked out his name, and only emptiness answered. Then her eyes fell upon the envelope propped up against his rumpled pillow.

She saw that white square of paper and that was the symbol of finality she had dreaded. He was gone, and he had left no more than an impersonal, polite, written goodbye... thanks for the ride.

Her hand trembled as she reached for it. She did not want to open it. As long as she didn't open it she could go on believing that there was still hope, that she had not given her heart only to have it returned in an unmarked envelope...

Shaking hands tore open the envelope. A folded sheet of paper and two fifty-dollar bills fell into her lap. For a long time she simply stared at it, the money lying against the white sheet like a condemnation, while something within her so newly brought to life slowly began to curl up and die. It was an ugly compulsion that made her unfold the letter, and it was a long time before she could make her eyes focus on the words.

Don't be an idiot, Dusty, take the money— you're going to need it to get settled. I wanted it to be more, but I knew how you would feel about accepting even this. This room is paid for in advance for a month; that should give you time to find a place of your own. Bob is expecting your call this morning; if he doesn't hear from you by noon he will call you.

You're a survivor, Dusty. I know you're going to make it. . . .

She had to stop there for a moment. Her chest seemed to be closing in on her lungs; she couldn't breathe. Her eyes were hot and dry, and over and over the words pounded, *You're a survivor, Dusty* . . . On the nightstand by the bed was the cactus in the paper cup that she had brought in last night with the rest of her belongings. Last night, when she had thought she would be spending the next days in this room along with him . . . *You're a survivor, Dusty* . . .

I wish for you small battles in peaceful places, a house with your own willow tree, and a life filled with green and growing things.

There were two more lines, four more words, and Dusty stared at them until the ink began to blur and the letters all ran together in a blue smear across the white paper. She stared at them until her heart finally broke with a slow, twisting, tearing motion, and the tears that flowed down her cheeks and blotched the paper were like drops of rain upon arid earth. The words were: I love you, Camp.

Chapter Twelve

Dusty paused before her desk, staring at the philodendron in the bright yellow pot that had not been there when she had gone home last night. "What in the world—?"

Sarah, her coworker at the next desk, looked up with a shrug and a smile. "I don't know. The florist was waiting when I got here this morning."

"Florist?" Dusty's cheeks tingled with delight as she searched for a card. There was none, and there could only be one possible explanation. She smiled happily to herself and went immediately to Bob's office.

Bob was a studious, wiry little man in his early thirties whose life completely revolved around his wife, Alice, and their six-month-old daughter. He had been Dusty's savior these past few months, and the gratitude and affection she felt for him were more than a simple employee-employer relationship. A gesture such as the one with the plant was typical of him.

In the end it had been he who had called her, a few minutes before noon as Dusty sat in the empty motel room in the numbness of shock that let hours slip by like minutes. It had been shock that had propelled her through the first interview, and through the first few days on her new job. Bob seemed to know everything about her without being told, he anticipated her needs and met them in simple ways without being asked. Once he had mentioned to her that he and Camp had gone to school together, and Camp's name had never come up again—but sometimes Dusty suspected the special treatment she was receiving from Bob was due to parting instructions from Camp. Or perhaps, she only wanted to believe that.

He had taken her home to meet his family; she had immediately fallen in love with the chubby baby and she and Alice were now fast friends. That in itself was a lifesaver to Dusty. Being with the happy family in their cozy suburban home, feeling the love and the unity and the good humor that flowed between them, and being made to feel a part of it had lifted her beyond the tragedy of the past and into a sense of peace with the present. She begged to babysit for them even when they did not want to go out, they laughingly indulged her, and the cheerful, indiscriminately affectionate little baby was now as much at home in Dusty's apartment as she was in her own room.

Alice and Bob had helped her find the apartment, a brightly furnished efficiency that was within her budget and on an easy bus route to the bank where she worked. Dusty and Alice had shopped for dishes and linens and all the personal accessories that made it home, and Dusty had known from the moment she had transplanted her cactus from the paper cup to a clay pot and set it in the windowsill that this *was* her home. She had found a place where she belonged.

Today marked the end of her three-month probationary period at the bank. Alice knew how much Dusty loved plants, Dusty had mentioned many times that she wanted to shop the nurseries to begin a collection as soon as she had time. It had probably been Alice's idea that Bob send her the philodendron as a way of saying congratulations on the end of her probation and the beginning of full-time permanent job status.

"Thanks," Dusty smiled, knocking on his open door. "I love philodendrons."

Bob looked up from his ledger, slightly distracted. "I'm glad. Thanks for what?"

Dusty was taken aback. "You didn't send the philodendron?"

He frowned, completely lost. "The what?"

"The plant," she stammered, confused. "I—I thought . . . well, since today is the end of my job probation, I thought it was your way of saying— you were pleased with my work and that I was being officially kept on . . ."

He shook his head, turning back to his papers. "Sorry. It was a nice thought, but I didn't have it."

She hesitated, looking at him uncertainly. Finally she ventured, "Does that mean—you're not pleased? That I'm..."

He looked up, once again confused, and when he saw the look on her face laughter sprang to his. "Honestly, Dusty, you are a walking tower of paranoia! Of course we're pleased," he assured her. "Of course you're being kept on—we have a job performance interview set up this afternoon with personnel to make it official. Convinced?"

She nodded, relieved, but after a moment the puzzled frown came back into her eyes. "I wonder who did send it then." she murmured.

"I've no idea," replied Bob without looking up from his work. "Some admirer, no doubt." And then he glanced at her. "You have a lot of them, you know."

Dusty did know, but the fact did not bother her as much as it once might have. Since coming here she had begun to let down her defenses—perhaps knowing that she was going to stay had made it easier for her to relax with people and make friends. She was unaware that it was her personality that attracted men as well as her appearance, but she was pleased to discover for the first time in her life that quite a few of the men she knew could actually be called friends and were not simply threatening objects to be avoided. She had been asked out many times, and she always refused, but she no longer felt that the men with whom she worked saw her only as an object for lewd glances and locker-room conversation. Had she changed, or had something about the world around her changed?

Still, it bothered her to think that one of her "admirers" had taken to sending anonymous gifts and she waited nervously all day for the phone call or the personal visit that would follow the flower. When none came she shrugged and dismissed it, accepting from her coworkers various explanations for the mystery which ranged from a lost card, to a mistaken delivery, to the shy teenager in the mailroom.

But the next day the philodendron on her desk was joined by an asparagus fern, and the plot thickened. Excitement buzzed around the accounting department when a flowering geranium arrived the following day. There were no cards and no one could get anything out of the florist. To her bored coworkers the entire thing began to take on the atmosphere of high drama, but for Dusty it was only mildly disturbing. This was beginning to take on the appearance of a dedicated campaign and she spent too many working hours reviewing in her mind which of the bank's male employees might be guilty of such underhanded persistence. Eventually she expanded that list to include her neighbors, a few men she had met at a barbecue at Alice and Bob's house at the end of the summer, even a Branch Manager whom she had never met, but with whom she talked on the phone every day and who, everyone assured her, must be at least sixty years old.

She took her collection home over the weekend and summarily dismissed the problem, only to have it resume again on Monday with a spray of coleus in a ceramic pot. On Tuesday there was a two-foot rubber tree, and the entire thing was starting to get out of hand. By Thursday an ornamental pepper plant and a small schefflera had been added, and Dusty's apartment was beginning to look like a green house. She could not fault the giver's taste, for she now had, with no effort or expense on her part, the final touches that would make her apartment a home, and she loved it. She became more and more anxious to learn the identity of her "secret admirer" but she was also worried. How could she turn down someone who had spent so much thought, effort, and expense upon winning her good favor? And who had, in all truth, succeeded quite admirably.

On Friday there was nothing, and Dusty tried to tell herself she was relieved. It was probably, after all, just some mix-up with the florist, and she would be lucky if she didn't get a bill at the end of the month that would take most of her paycheck.

And then, just as she was locking up her desk for the weekend, she glanced up from the lower drawer and saw a small cactus in a clay pot upon her desk. The pot was attached to a lean brown hand, above it was a wrist encased in cordovan leather, and she could make her eyes go no farther.

A voice, as soft as silk, as familiar as her own heartbeat, floated down to her. "Hello, Dusty."

She couldn't seem to move her eyes from the cactus. Three months. Three months in which to become part of the new life he had given her, three months in which she had convinced herself she had gotten over him... what choice had she had? She would never forget him, this man who had shown her love and changed her life, always a part of her would be inextricably linked with him, but he had left her and she had had no choice but to go on living... She looked at the cactus and she realized consciously what she had always known but had been afraid to hope for. Her own voice strained and hoarse, echoed the one word, "Camp."

She made her eyes look up, over lean hips and thighs encased in brown corduroy, a tawny-colored sweater covered by the brown leather jacket, the familiar face and light hair.... Familiar, yet different. The desert tan had faded, his face looked older, more mature. The rugged hair was neatly, yet casually, styled, his face was sober and his eyes a very dark blue. In those eyes was a hint of anxiety, a slight uneasiness, and a spark of something indefinable when he looked at her that made her heart, numb and lifeless with shock, leap suddenly into a startling, painfully joyous rhythm. Camp. It *was* him. He was here, before her, the embodiment of too many restless yearning dreams which had ended in a cold awakening in an empty bed... real and solid and standing here before her. Camp. The pulsing of her heart in her chest was a strange and unfamiliar sensation... as though, before this moment, it had never beat at all.

His eyes swept over her, lightening by degrees as they took in every detail—her wavy hair pulled away from her face by two ivory barrettes, her bright pink blouse and simple black skirt, her face, now stunned and expressionless, her slender throat, the one hand with its neatly manicured and buffed nails that fluttered uncertainly on her desk and he drew in his breath automatically. "Dusty," he said softly. "You look wonderful."

Camp. The sudden rushing pulse of blood through her veins, the pounding in her ears, even the rhythm of her breath which was oddly light and uneven, seemed to echo that word. Eagerly drinking him in, his lean, strong form, the smooth face, the streaked blond hair, even the familiar scent of his aftershave—hardly daring to believe it, gradually accepting it, and then slowly overwhelmed by a question that choked in her throat almost before she could ask it... "But—but—what are you doing here?"

He tried to smile, the smile died even as it touched his lips. There was an uneasiness in his eyes and in his tone and his voice was husky as he said, "You're going to think I've got a hell of a nerve..." But then, suddenly restless, he looked about the room, at the clock on the wall, at the keys in her hand. He said abruptly, "Were you getting ready to leave? Is there somewhere we can go to talk?"

She hesitated for only a moment, then nodded. They walked out of the building together, out into the fading multicolored September day, and she hesitated for only a moment before volunteering, "Would you like to see my apartment?" She wanted very much for him to see it, for it was greatly due to him that she had it, it almost belonged to him as much as it did to her.

He smiled, and for the moment that his eyes caught hers the spark of sheer happiness there ignited a reciprocal emotion in her that was almost too great to be borne. "I'd like that," he said, and he touched her arm to lead her toward a red Volvo parked at the curb.

There she hesitated. "Is this yours?"

He opened the door for her. "Umm-hmm." And to the question in her eyes he answered, "I sold the rig. I'll explain it to you later, Dusty. I have a lot to explain to you," he added soberly, and she sat back, so absorbed in digesting this information that she forgot to give him directions to her apartment. She was surprised to look up a few minutes later to find they were almost there.

"How did you know which way to go?" she inquired.

"I've talked to Bob," he answered, still rather enigmatically. "He's been keeping me up to date on things."

She hardly knew what to make of this, either. He had been in touch with Bob, all this time... Bob had never mentioned anything to her. He had talked to Bob—to keep up with her? Why? And why hadn't he called her? Why had he just disappeared without a word?... She frowned, unable to contain her curiosity a moment longer. "Bob never mentioned that he had heard from you," she said.

"I asked him not to." Camp pulled up in front of her apartment building and looked at her. His smile was reassuring, seeming to ask for her patience while at the same moment promising all her questions would be answered. He was asking her to trust him one more time.

She was nervous as she took out her keys and opened the door. Dusty wanted him to like this little place that she had made her home. She wanted him to know that it was a part of him and of all he had helped her to become, and that no matter how long she lived here or how much she loved it, it would never be complete until he stood inside the threshold.

His eyes swept slowly over the whole, taking in the few carefully chosen yet integral personal touches that made the room uniquely hers—the fabric she had chosen for the curtains and cushions in pale etchings of spring-green and rose-pink on white, the landscape prints, the butterfly coasters and ceramic ash trays, the plants he had sent her which finally made it home. When he turned to her his smile was soft and adoring. "Funny," he said quietly. "It's exactly the way I imagined it." And his voice was husky as he added, "I've imagined it often, Dusty. You wouldn't believe how often."

She wanted then to run into his arms, to hold him and to never let him go, and the small, almost unnoticeable movement he made toward her told her he wanted the same thing. But caution held her back, caution and uncertainty, and she said quickly, "Do you want some coffee?"

"No." His voice was quiet, his eyes shaded as he reached for her hand. "Could we just sit down—and talk for a minute?"

Her hand rested willingly inside his and he drew her to the sofa. He sat there beside her for a long moment without speaking, simply holding her hand, and through the questions and uncertainties that cascaded through Dusty was the simple awareness of how right her hand felt resting inside his strong, warm one. It felt so right that nothing else mattered then, his absence, his unexpected return, the explanations he seemed so reluctant to make... if only he would go on sitting beside her like this, and holding her hand.

Then he began to speak. "I've been in Boston these last three months," he said. And her surprised look met a painful apology in his. "I couldn't tell you, Dusty, I couldn't—do anything until I knew how things were going to work out there. I wanted to." His breath was short and harsh, she felt his muscles tense next to hers as he dropped his eyes and said lowly, "The hardest thing I ever did in my life was walk away from you that morning..." Her heart began to pump an erratic, hope-infusing rhythm, and his smile was wan as he glanced back at her. "Facing my father, the charges, the bar association—it was all child's play after that," he assured her.

She searched his face anxiously, hardly daring to believe what he was saying, yearning to believe what she saw in his eyes...eyes that met hers with tenderness and need, that traveled slowly over her face and rested upon her lips with a sudden flare of urgency. She whispered, mesmerized by that look and her own intense yearning, "What happened?"

His eyes dropped to the hand he held within his, the slow breath he took was deliberately calming. "It wasn't as bad as I expected," he admitted. "It just took some time. The worst part..." Again he looked at her, and the longing in his eyes broke her heart. "Was not being able to tell you. I couldn't, Dusty," he said softly, urgently. "I couldn't ask anything of you, I couldn't promise you anything, until I was sure I had something to offer you. Can you please understand that? You had been hurt so often, you had had so many of your dreams stolen...how could I ask you to give up everything again to live the life of a fugitive with me?"

He took another short breath, he dropped his eyes again. "Anyway," he continued, more calmly, "as I said it took some time, but everything is finally legally and officially clear. The charges against me were dropped, and my father..." He glanced at her with a small, rather wistful smile. "Life with my family has never been reruns of *Leave It to Beaver*, but at least my dad and I are communicating now. We've reached an understanding. I suppose we both just had some growing up to do. And of course . . ." Anxiety crept into his eyes. "Now that I've cleared things with the Massachusetts Bar Association I'm free to apply for a license to practice in other states . . . like Pennsylvania, for instance." There was a quickening in the depths of his eyes, a new anxiety. "You do like it here, don't you?"

Dusty couldn't speak. A sudden joy had leaped to her throat and lodged there, her head was whirling and she couldn't think, she couldn't speak. Her world had suddenly been tilted and shaken around and returned to her with all that she had ever wanted, hers for the grasping and she couldn't believe it. She could only stare at him helplessly and speechlessly, and even when she saw the pain creep into his eyes she could do nothing to reassure him.

His face was taut with misery and a hint of desperate determination, his fingers tightened on hers even though his voice was heavy with defeat. "I know I have no right to ask this of you," he said. "You have your life the way you want it now—I left you with no reason to think I would ever come back . . . But don't you see I had to do that, Dusty?" He pleaded. His grip on her hand was painful, but the happiness and the euphoria that flooded her was so great she did not feel it. "I don't want to change your life," he insisted. "I don't want to take away anything you have or interfere with anything you want for yourself . . . I only want to share it—to help, sometimes, if I can." His breath was long and somewhat unsteady. "Dusty," he said quietly, "I think I loved you the minute I saw you fighting for survival against odds three times your size ... everything I discovered about you only made me love you more. Before I knew it you were part of me, so much so that sometimes I couldn't tell where I left off and you began. I tried to leave you in Santa Fe. I tried to leave my love for you behind in the Texas desert ... I knew it was already too late. Dusty ..." His eyes were uncertain, desperately pleading behind a mask of calmness, and he said evenly, "I want to share that house in the suburbs with you. I want to put a swing set up on the lawn for our kids and I want to plant the willow tree with you. Do you ..." His eyes searched hers hesitantly, his voice fell almost to a whisper. "Do you still want me?"

She slowly pulled her hand away. She had to turn her face because the tears that had flooded her eyes were threatening to spill and after a moment she said, thickly, "I think you were right. You have a hell of a nerve."

She heard his sharp intake of breath, and upon it she turned. The pain and disappointment in his face slowly turned to wonder as he saw her eyes, bright with unshed tears, and her face glowing with love and pride, as she brought her hand up to caress his cheek and she whispered, "Camp, I know how hard it was for you to go back. I know how much it cost you—"

His eyes still anxiously searched her face, hardly daring to believe it, his breathing was unsteady as he interrupted, "It wasn't hard at all—once I found something worth facing it for. It didn't cost me anything...as long as I could have you. Oh, Dusty—"

And unable to restrain themselves any longer, they were in each other's arms, her whisper broken against his face and his lips, "Yes...Oh, yes!..."

And later, lying in each other's arms in the tangle of the linens of her own bed, she murmured, "Children...did you say children?"

"Hmm?" He lay absently twining her hair about his finger, lost in dreams of his own.

She looked up at him. "The swing set. For our own children?"

He looked down at her, the happiness that swelled within him growing in his eyes and spilling into the tightening of his embrace as he drew her closer and closer, as though he could never have enough. "As many as you want," he promised. "A real family...for both of us."

Her lips reached his, their shared touch and deepening joy lifting them both to the beginnings of renewed passion, and then she lifted her face, a small puzzled frown whispering across her brow. "Camp...do willow trees grow in Philadelphia?"

He smiled, his hand cupping her face as his lips touched and treasured a slow path across every inch of it. "Darling," he answered softly, "I am firmly convinced that they would grow in the desert"—his lips brushed across her cheek, the tip of her nose, and to the corner of her mouth—"if you planted them there."

And surrendering to the passion that flowered within them like the bud of joy, they melted into one another. Throughout the night they dreamed a single dream; a new day dawned on the beginning of life, and still they clung together ... content, peaceful, at home at last.

BARBARA DELINSKY
Fingerprints

Carly Quinn is a
woman with a past.
Born Robyn Hart, she
was forced to don a new
identity when her intensive
investigation of an arson-ring
resulted in a photographer's death
and threats against her life.

Ryan Cornell's entrance into her life
was a gradual one. The handsome
lawyer's interest was piqued, and then
captivated, by the mysterious Carly—a
woman of soaring passions and a
secret past.

Harlequin Stationery Offer

Personalized Rainbow Memo Pads for you or a friend

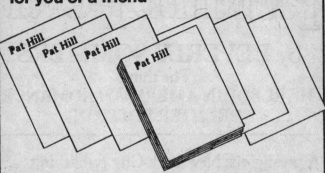

Picture your name in bold type at the top of these attractive rainbow memo pads. Each 4¼" x 5½" pad contains 150 rainbow sheets—yellow, pink, gold, blue, buff and white—enough to last you through months of memos. Handy to have at home or office.

Just clip out three proofs of purchase (coupon below) from an August or September release of Harlequin Romance, Harlequin Presents, Harlequin Superromance, Harlequin American Romance, Harlequin Temptation or Harlequin Intrigue and add $4.95 (includes shipping and handling), and we'll send you *two* of these attractive memo pads imprinted with your name.

Harlequin Stationery Offer
(PROOF OF PURCHASE)

NAME_____

(Please Print)

ADDRESS_____

CITY_____STATE_____ZIP_____

NAME ON STATIONERY_____

Mail 3 proofs of purchase, plus check or money order for $4.95 payable to:	Harlequin Books P.O. Box 52020 Phoenix, AZ 85072	4-3

Offer expires December 31, 1984. (Not available in Canada)   STAT-1

RIDE A PAINTED PONY

by BEVERLY SOMMERS
The third
HARLEQUIN AMERICAN ROMANCE
PREMIER EDITION

A prestigious New York City publishing
company decides to launch a new historical
romance line, led by a woman who must first
define what love means.

Enter a uniquely exciting new world with

Harlequin American Romance™

Harlequin American Romances are the first romances to explore today's love relationships. These compelling novels reach into the hearts and minds of women across America... probing the most intimate moments of romance, love and desire.

You'll follow romantic heroines and irresistible men as they boldly face confusing choices. Career first, love later? Love without marriage? Long-distance relationships? All the experiences that make love real are captured in the tender, loving pages of **Harlequin American Romances**.

What makes American women so different when it comes to love? Find out with **Harlequin American Romance!**

Send for your introductory FREE book now!

Get this book FREE!

Harlequin American Romance

Twice in a Lifetime
REBECCA FLANDERS

Mail to:

Harlequin Reader Service

In the U.S.
2504 West Southern Ave.
Tempe, AZ 85282

In Canada
P.O. Box 2800, Postal Station A
5170 Yonge St., Willowdale, Ont. M2N 5T5

YES! I want to be one of the first to discover **Harlequin American Romance.** Send me FREE and without obligation *Twice in a Lifetime.* If you do not hear from me after I have examined my FREE book, please send me the 4 new **Harlequin American Romances** each month as soon as they come off the presses. I understand that I will be billed only $2.25 for each book (total $9.00). There are no shipping or handling charges. There is no minimum number of books that I have to purchase. In fact, I may cancel this arrangement at any time. *Twice in a Lifetime* is mine to keep as a FREE gift, even if I do not buy any additional books.

154-BPA-NAXE

Name   (please print)

Address   Apt. no.

City   State/Prov.   Zip/Postal Code

Signature (If under 18, parent or guardian must sign.)

This offer is limited to one order per household and not valid to current Harlequin American Romance subscribers. We reserve the right to exercise discretion in granting membership. If price changes are necessary, you will be notified.

Offer expires January 31, 1985.

AMR-SUB-2